This book was edited and formatted by the author. All artwork was generated by AI.

J. B. Jefferson
maigosmemories@gmail.com
@MaigosMemories

METANOIA PT. 1: MAIGO'S REBIRTH

J. B. JEFFERSON

Metanoia is the story of a boy unraveling the system designed to shape him—one soul-crushing lesson at a time.

To my dearest grandmother.

TABLE OF CONTENTS

STEEL BRACELETS   PG. 5

THE OASIS   PG. 54

CHASING THE DRAGON   PG. 94

SURVIVAL INSTINCTS   PG. 143

THE FPM   PG. 181

TERRA'S TUNDRA   PG. 208

MAIGO'S REBIRTH   PG. 240

SYLVAIN'S CHAMPION   PG. 265

A MOMENT WITH MASTER   PG. 288

ABOUT THE AUTHOR   PG. 303

Chapter 1

STEEL BRACELETS

T he last time I had a decent night's sleep, I was too young to remember. I don't mean the kind where you toss and turn or wake up sweating—I mean real, undisturbed sleep. That kind disappeared when I was still a kid.

It's not that I can't sleep. I can. I do. But I always wake up exhausted. My dreams make sure of that. They're vivid, twisted things, too sharp to be random, too cruel to be coincidence. Some come and go like whispers in the dark, but others latch onto my skull like parasites. The worst ones happen before something in my life takes a turn. Like a warning, only useless.

Last night's was one of those.

I was walking through an endless cavern, the air thick with silence. My own footsteps were the only sound, but they didn't feel like mine. The more I walked, the more the tunnels looked the same—just empty voids stretching infinitely. Then I saw it: a dead end, carved with a glyph that pulsed with a sickly glow. It looked like a dragon, coiled in some grotesque stance, its eyes black pits of nothing. I don't know why I reached out. Maybe boredom. Maybe desperation.

But the moment my fingers brushed the glyph, light exploded, blinding. A thunderous roar filled the cave, a sound so deep and layered it wasn't just noise—it was inside me, rattling my teeth, crawling beneath my skin. Then, without warning, the dragon inhaled, sucking the air from the world. I felt my chest collapse, my head splitting open from the pressure. Just as the darkness swallowed me whole—

BZZZZZZZT.

My body lurched awake, my mind still clawing its way out of the dream.

"*Good morning, Maigo,*" Omi chimed, his synthetic voice infuriatingly cheerful. "*It is seven-*

thirty a.m., Thursday, April fourteenth, twenty
ninety-two. Class starts at nine a.m. Time to get out
of bed."

He repeated the sentence like a looping
emergency broadcast. It made me want to smash
my head through the nearest surface.

I groaned. *"I hate my life."*

*"That is an unfortunate perspective,
Master Maigo. Would you like to hear your
schedule for today?"*

"I do the same thing every day."

*"You had some strange dreams last
night."* Omi didn't "laugh," but he had ways of
making it sound like he was enjoying himself.

"Did you make the dragon appear?" I
muttered. *"Do I need to tell mom to limit your
permissions again?"*

*"Dragon? I have no idea what you're
talking about."* He paused. *"By the way, you've
been enrolled in the V9 Program for the rest of the
school year. Congratulations!"*

*"Hopefully, that'll get me time away from
you."*

"How rude, Master Maigo!"

I ignored him and forced myself out of bed, my body heavy with fatigue. *The V9 Program.* I barely even remembered taking the test, and I sure as hell didn't sign up for it voluntarily. The school had made me. I'd even tried answering the test questions like a complete idiot just to fail on purpose, but somehow, I'd been accepted anyway.

It felt inevitable. Like someone had already decided this was going to happen. To me, the world always seemed that way. Like there was some top-tier movie director making decisions for me. Like everything that happened was in the hands of a hidden, master puppeteer whose strings can't be seen, felt, or -most of all- escaped. Like my life was this ultimate theatrical production to entertain a lonely being, far more twisted than myself, and everyone I knew was just the underpaid acting staff.

Mom told me thoughts like that were dangerous and that I should keep them to myself. She always said things like "don't say anything in school that you didn't learn there," and "you should smile, people would like you more." It's not like she was perfect. If you really looked closely, you could

8

catch glimpses of the monster hiding beneath her facade.

Despite her very real flaws, she sure loved pretending to be little-miss-rosey-shit in public, and people loved her. She'd just regurgitate statements that she'd heard on The Daily News to keep her friends entertained. Sometimes she threw small events in the community, where she would politic with the local authorities and make it known how much she subscribes to the public consensus.

On the other hand, she was raising a local delinquent. I don't watch The Daily News, and I don't talk to people. Maybe she was just compensating for my rebellious nature. I couldn't bring myself to say or do anything I didn't believe in. That just wasn't the type of person I wanted to be and this caused some distance between us.

By the time I made it to the kitchen, my mother was standing at the counter, flipping maple sausage with methodical precision. Her eyes were clear, her posture perfect, her movements smooth. The ideal image of a functioning, responsible adult.

"Good morning, Maigo," she said, like we were strangers. "Did you sleep well?"

"I was dreaming about the cave again."

She didn't react. She never did. Instead, she kept her attention on the pan. "Want eggs?"

That was how it always went. She never addressed the things that mattered. I could tell her I watched someone get shot in the street, and she'd ask if I wanted juice or water with my toast.

"No, thanks."

I grabbed a banana and turned to leave, but as I passed her, I took notice of another all too familiar nightmare.

Her sleeves were long today.

She always did that, when she used. Covered her arms. Made sure the tremors weren't visible when she handed me something. She wasn't reckless. She was careful, precise. She knew how to function. How to make it seem like nothing was wrong. Her addiction wasn't loud, and wasn't messy. It was silent, efficient. It never got in the way of her work, never tarnished the image of the perfect professional. No one suspected a thing. No one could.

Except me.

"You seem a bit sluggish." My voice was neutral, hinting suspicion.

She quickly glanced at me, her expression unreadable. "I didn't sleep much last night."

That was a lie. She'd slept fine—after knocking herself into oblivion with whatever she was taking now. But I didn't call her out. I never did. It wouldn't change anything.

"Are you sure you're okay?" I couldn't hide the concern in my voice.

"Oh, don't worry honey! I just haven't had my caffeine yet." She wouldn't dare share her burden with me.

"I'm heading out," I said, shoving the banana into my bag.

"Be careful."

That part always sounded real.

Outside, the world was sterile and suffocating.

Los Mitos was a fortress of concrete and metal, built in rings like a great machine, each layer serving a purpose. The outermost ring—military

bases, cybernetic research, security. The next—
factories, production plants, the backbone of the
city's economy. The middle—residential districts,
education labs, where the youth were processed
into society's machine.

Everything was efficient. Everything had
a place. And people like me? We were being
molded into whatever role they wanted us to fill.
Each cog played its designated role, in perfect
harmony and rhythm. It always felt so surreal. The
way the gardening old lady, two houses down,
always waved to me at the same time. The way the
hovers danced around the sky, like a hive of wasps,
as people made their way to work. The way the
billboards always switched to that video of Sylvain's
"heroic moment," right as I turned the corner and it
became visible. I hated that one.

That comic book style orange and yellow
background didn't match the content. That cheesy
arc-shot camera angle circling the two men was
beyond distasteful. It was like a parody, with none
of the irony to balance the cringe. The way it cut
between close ups of Sylvain, and the enemy
leader on his knees begging for mercy made me
nauseated. Then. Boom. He blows his head

completely off his shoulders. Fade to black. Then some sort've praise for the Atlas General. I'd seen that video every day since I started high school. My stomach turned for the middle school kid ten strides ahead of me in awe of what he'd seen.

A few blocks away from school, I saw a man getting arrested.

It happened fast. One minute he was walking down the street, the next a fleet of camouflaged hovers descended on him like vultures.

The P.O.s moved in perfect unison, yanking him away from the walkway, slamming him into the pavement. The smallest officer struck him twice in the ribs, each hit landing with a dull, sickening thud.

Then I saw it. His necklace.

A single symbol hung from the chain, catching the light.

Akoma Ntoso.

It meant "linked hearts." I'd watched my father get the same one tattooed on his arm. The grit on his face told me the pain was worth burning it into his flesh. I never understood why it was so important. I just know he disappeared a few weeks later and every time I saw it I couldn't help but think of him.

My heart turned to ice. The officers were saying something. I wasn't listening. I was too busy staring. Too busy remembering.

One of the larger officers noticed me watching. He started toward me.

"Let's make our way to school before they take you too!" Omi's voice cut through my panic.

I turned and walked. Fast. I didn't stop until I was through the school gates. And even then, I couldn't shake the feeling that someone had **seen** me. The constant anxiety of being a beggar haunted me.

"Beggars are publicly shamed."

"Beggars get taken away by P.Os."

"Beggars don't get to grow up and be somebody."

Atlas General Sylvain says beggars are a cancer on society. "With such a finite lifespan, no man should call from his knees for a fictional being to bring him salvation," his famous quote painted on the wall above my locker.

"I'm only sixteen. Why should I live in fear, just because of my beliefs?" Hell, I wasn't even sure what I believed at the time. They just took away my right to find out who I wanted to be. But I had to play my role. And most of all, I had to keep it to myself.

I got to school earlier than usual and spent a few minutes circling the courtyard, trying to piece together what I'd seen on the walk. That man in the street, beaten and dragged away like livestock. The Akoma Ntoso pendant that mirrored my father's tattoo. The look on the officer's face when he noticed me watching.

It wasn't fear I felt. Not really. It was something heavier. Something that sank. Despair. An endless dark tunnel, with a nightmarish light waiting for me at the end. Why would I keep going? I didn't get far into those thoughts before they were interrupted.

"Maigo! Come check out my new boost!" Yoen's voice. Loud, reckless, and just a bit more devious than usual.

I turned to find him jogging over with a ridiculous grin plastered across his pale, wind-burnt face. His skin was dry and stretched tight over sharp features, and that god-awful bowl cut made him look like a big kindergartener.

"Great," I muttered. "The spirit of chaos arrives."

He ignored me and threw a fist bump—his new hand buzzing faintly against mine. The metal was cool, but the pulse of electricity under the skin made my stomach twist.

"One of the older kids in my lab is a goddamn artist with augments," Yoen said, proudly flexing the new graft. "I know. I know. Completely illegal. But totally worth it. Watch this." He closed his eyes. "Is Omi online?"

"Every morning, like sentient-AI clockwork," I said dryly.

"*Some people would appreciate such a timely companion,*" Omi replied, predictably.

Yoen smiled, placed his hand on my head —and suddenly I felt it. A flicker of static. A pinprick of heat.

"Oh, Master Maigo, I don't feel so goo—"

Silence.

Omi went dark.

It was like someone had yanked the rain cloud from above my head.

I blinked. "Yoen. You—"

"Scrambled him." He grinned wider. "You're welcome. You're untraceable now. No eye in the sky, no behavioral logging, no records of our charming little rendezvous. If we wanna go off-grid, we're ghosts!"

I stared at him. "You grafted your hand... to hack police surveillance?"

He shrugged at my less than ideal reaction. "For you, bro."

A second later, he tapped my temple and brought Omi back online.

"Wha—what happened? Diagnostic inconsistency detected..."

"Don't worry, Omi," Yoen said, tapping my head with his unaltered hand. "If you can hear me in there, I was just kidding. Won't happen again."

I should've felt grateful. But instead I felt… unmoored. Like a thread had been plucked in the back of my mind, one that was never meant to be touched.

Then Yoen hit me with another bomb. "Oh yeah—guess who your V9 partner is?"

I groaned. "Yeah. Omi told me. Thanks for the warning."

"At least it's me and not just some drone-eyed valedictorians," Yoen said. "You should be hyped. We're the second cohort to ever try this. You know how elite that is? Somebody up there saw something in us, Maigo."

He said it with an awe I couldn't match. I dodged a bullet with the alarm bells. "Let's head to class."

"If we crush this program, they might pick us for the summer iteration. That means higher clearance, advanced tech, maybe even placement into actual field units."

"Right," I muttered. "Because nothing screams 'summer fun' like military-sponsored psychological experimentation."

"You don't even care." Yoen hung his head and fell in step beside me as we walked.

"Still don't get why they picked me," I said. "They say the whole point of V9 is to make genius engineers or next-gen biofuel chemists. Me? I'm just good at noticing bullshit and pretending to care."

"You're better than you think," Yoen repostured, "which is exactly why you scare them."

Omi chimed in, his voice strained. *"Master Maigo, I must remind you—I have full access to your memory logs. Such self-deprecation could trigger behavioral review."*

"Shut up before I have Yoen fry your brains again." I said out loud.

Yoen beamed. "You do love me."

We descended into the lower levels of the school, where the air grew colder, heavier—like the building itself knew we were heading somewhere we weren't meant to be. Room 003 was at the very end of a forgotten corridor, buried behind two outdated storage rooms. We stepped inside.

Silence.

The room was sterile and dimly lit, and I instantly locked eyes on the machines in the back —eight enormous chrome coffins lined against the far wall, their surfaces polished to the point of surrealism.

Each one bore the inscription:

PROJECT TAUR V9 – LEARNING CHEST

The words shimmered slightly, as if the metal itself was breathing. I stepped closer, inspecting the inner chamber of the nearest unit. Smooth. Seamless. Impersonal. Like something meant to hold bodies, not minds.

"Named after Dr. Taur I think," Yoen muttered. "He was the first to design mind-assimilation protocols, right?"

"Yeah." I nodded. "Then he vanished. And nobody really looked for him."

That part stuck with me. A man who built a machine to erase the line between cognition and simulation disappeared—and they just let him go like that. I couldn't buy it.

The room had two long tables positioned like interrogation benches. One was already filled— two boys and two girls, all upperclassmen, all unnervingly quiet. They didn't look at us. Didn't smile. Just sat there like statues, like they'd already been through something and came back... altered. At the other table, two girls from our year were seated on opposite ends with a wide silence between them.

Terra Waters sat on the far left. Of course she did. Everything about her was composed, sharp. The kind of girl who didn't just get perfect grades—she made the teachers feel stupid. Ever since we were kids, I've been obsessed with her. Her blue eyes were unsettling, not just because they were pretty, but because they looked like they saw through things. Like they could dismantle a person if they kept her gaze too long. Endless brown hair fell down her back, seemingly growing as you stared at it. We'd hooked up once. Months before. Since then, she'd vanished from my orbit without a trace. I never knew why. And now she was here.

The other girl was Jade Cohen, our school's own androgynous war machine. She was cut from stone—broad shoulders, bionic ankles (though she'd never admit it), and a reputation for ending any race, fight, or argument before it started. Yoen had been obsessed with her since last year. Which meant I was about to witness a tragedy.

We took the empty seats between them. I sat beside Terra and gave her a nod. She returned a thin, unreadable smile. Yoen, naturally, chose to sit beside Jade. He nodded once—cool, casual. She reached out and crushed his hand in a handshake that rattled the table.

Yoen hissed through his teeth. "I think I just lost a knuckle."

"You'll live," Jade said, deadpan.

A moment later, the door hissed open. Two men walked in—one in a sharp black suit, the other in a white lab coat. Dr. Cobb. and Dr. Light. I'd seen their names in orientation files. Never expected them to look like corporate recruiters at a funeral.

Cobb walked to the podium and clasped his hands like he was preparing for a theatrical monologue. Light went to the machines and started pressing commands into a control panel with surgical precision. A deep hum filled the room—the machines were alive.

"Good morning, students," Cobb began. His voice was too smooth, too rehearsed. "I am Dr. Indus Cobb. My associate, Dr. Avin Light, and I will be your guides through the V9 Learning Experience. I will be with you inside the simulations. He will remain out here, monitoring your physical integrity."

He paused and scanned the room. We weren't students. We were subjects.

Cobb began pacing. "Before we continue, I welcome any initial questions."

Four hands went up.

He pointed lazily at one of the seniors—a twitchy kid with a sunken face and jerking fingers.

"G-g-good morning. I'm Jace. I was wondering… w-why do our bodies need to be monitored? Are the machines d-dangerous?"

The air in the room stilled.

Cobb smiled. "An excellent question, Jace. The Learning Chests are completely safe. Dr.

Light is here to ensure your vitals remain stable, that's all."

The other hands dropped. No one else wanted to be noticed.

Cobb picked up again, pacing slower now, drawing us in like a magician about to reveal the trick. "Project Taur was built on a revolutionary idea: that experience is the most effective form of learning. Not textbooks, not lectures—immersion." He let the word linger, softly waving his hands to match the drawn out cadence, then reclasped them. "Dr. Taur, before his… unfortunate disappearance, developed neural-link technology capable of inserting your consciousness into simulations so real, they become part of your memory architecture. The events you experience in V9 will feel real. Pain, fear, triumph, grief—real. But I must emphasize, they are only simulations."

I felt my throat tighten.

"Are they?"

Cobb's smile flickered for a fraction of a second. Then he continued. "There are three principles you must remember during your time in the V9 program."

He raised a finger. "One: Lessons are expansive. They may draw inspiration from previous ones." Two fingers. "Two: Lessons may contain hidden tasks. Completing them earns influence. Sometimes... control." His eyes locked onto mine as he raised the third finger. "Three: The program does not end until the lesson is complete."

The words rang in my head like a closing door.

"Okay!" Cobb clapped once. "Seniors, to the back. Juniors, with me."

We stood and filed out of our seats. I felt the eyes of the upperclassmen as they passed us. Not friendly. Not welcoming. Just... cold.

At the back of the room, the Learning Chests sat open like hungry mouths. Jade was the first to climb in. She didn't hesitate. Yoen followed, grinning like he was about to play a game. Terra looked pale. She turned back toward the podium, toward Cobb. She didn't say anything, but I could see the panic in her eyes. That made me hesitate.

I stared at the open chest in front of me, the wires twitching slightly, like veins.

"Master Maigo," Omi said. *"During the simulation, I will be deactivated. The V9 environment cannot support dual operating systems."*

"Great."

I climbed in.

The moment the lid closed, the cold pierced straight through me.

The inside of the Learning Chest wasn't like the clinical cold of a hospital or a winter morning. This was the kind of cold that bit through skin and curled into bone, like the machine itself hated that I was still breathing. Electricity coursed through my body—sharp, blinding. I couldn't move. Couldn't scream. Then came the gas. It hissed down from a hidden valve above, and I felt my thoughts starting to slide off themselves, dissolving.

My last clear memory was the sound of Dr. Light's voice behind glass, saying something like "Here we go."

Then came the void. I wasn't sure if I was falling or floating, but I was weightless—trapped in a black nothingness so complete I couldn't tell where my body ended. Panic surged through me, but even that felt distant. Like it was happening to someone else. And just as quickly, it melted.

I felt… peace.

A fake kind of peace. Chemical, designed. Like someone had scrubbed my brain with warm water and dressed it in a hospital gown. I floated in that false calm until I heard them—

Laughter.

Playful. Human. Familiar.

Then color returned, like a sunrise bleeding into me. A pulse of pure red. Then orange. Then gold. They stretched across the sky until the blackness broke open, and the illusion of a world began to build itself. Trees. Birds. A breeze so gentle it almost felt sacred. A warm field. An empty campsite.

And Yoen's face—grinning like an idiot— popped into frame. "Maigo, wake up!" he shouted. "They're coming! Hurry up—they're coming!"

I panicked and scrambled upright, heart pounding—only to realize it was a joke. The field was empty. The sky too calm.

Yoen was doubled over, laughing.

Jade appeared next to him and reached down to help me up. "Don't listen to him," she muttered. "His brain didn't finish uploading."

Before I could say anything, a sudden beam of light struck the ground beside us.

A hologram of Dr. Cobb flickered into form, hands folded behind his back. "Hello, class, and welcome to your first lesson," he said, too calm, too delighted. "Normally, this particular exercise is completed in opposition. But today, due to the absence of one of your classmates, we've adapted the scenario so that you may all work together. Marvelous." His tone shifted. "You are on a plantation in Virginia. The year is 1820. Your objective: reach New York City, and meet me at this building."

A large building with stained-glass windows appeared in my hand, printed across a strange card.

"Do not die. And above all—do not get caught." The hologram vanished, leaving a ghastly sound bite behind. "I'll be watching.."

Yoen spun around and clapped his hands like a kid about to start a party. "Okay! Everybody relax. I am a VR god. I beat the entire Third Ward Voyage series in one weekend."

I rolled my eyes. "You say that like it's not embarrassing."

Then the earth buckled. The world shook, violently. I dropped to my hands and knees. One by one, the other students disappeared into flickers of static. The image of the campsite unraveled. My vision blurred and faded to black. My body compressed into nothingness again. The warm peace from earlier was gone.

I opened my eyes to the sun, and pain. Heat blistered across my skin. The sky above was wide and vicious, the light too bright to bear. The air smelled like wet burlap, sour sweat, and scorched timber. Every breath felt contaminated with pollen thick enough to chew and swallow. I was laid on my side, probably recuperating from a heat stroke. Behind, a man stood over me, pale and tall, casting a jagged shadow that split the dirt in half.

He wore a smirk and held a whip coiled in his hand. "Do you hear me talking, boy?"My mouth moved before I could think. "Of course, I—"

The whip cracked through the air and across my back. Pain erupted, not simulated—not distant. It was real. My body jolted. My hands reached behind me instinctively. Then I saw them. Not my hands.

Larger. Rough. Blackened skin. Fingernails cracked and thick.

My stomach dropped.

I tried to stand upright, to shake off the crawling fear under my skin, but the body I wore resisted. My back stayed bowed, hips tight, shoulders rounded inward like a question mark. This wasn't just a posture. It was a survival instinct, carved deep into muscle and marrow long before I ever arrived. I wasn't just pretending to be someone else — I was trapped in a life I didn't build but still had to survive.

I tried to speak again—tried to hold onto my own voice. "Sir, I would appreciate it if you'd—"

Another whip. Another scream.

The man's voice was trembling with rage. "Have you been readin', boy?"

I looked around and noticed everyone pretending to work. Too afraid to watch what was happening directly.

My brain caught up.

"Slaves weren't allowed to be educated."

I opened my mouth to answer — clean, clear words at the ready — but they snagged in my throat. Too clean. Too proud. I saw it in the overseer's squint, the way he leaned forward like a predator catching the scent of danger. I forced the words to slip and stumble on my tongue. "Naw suh... ain't done no book learnin'." The accent was jagged, broken — a cage I had to willingly step inside.

I closed my eyes expecting another lash.

He stared at me for a beat too long, then turned and walked back toward his horse.

I was shaking. Covered in sweat. The smell of iron and salt and dirt stuck to my skin like regret. I bent down and grabbed a half-empty sack and began picking. The simulation didn't just make me wear some else's skin. It made me wear their chains too. Out of the corner of my eye, I caught movement. An older man, shoulders trembling, dropped a bundle of cotton. He tried to scoop it back up, but he was too slow. The whip cracked once. The sound didn't just split the air. It fractured the world into "before" and "after." No one looked. No one even flinched. This was normal here. A rule of survival carved into every hunched back. Keep your head down. Keep your hands moving. Keep breathing.

A whisper came from the row beside me. "You should be more careful, Maigo."

I turned and stared.

An old woman stood hunched over a cotton bush. Her hands moved automatically, but her eyes were sharp. Familiar.

"Jade?" I whispered.

She didn't smile. Just nodded once.

The boy beside her shot me a sharp glance. "Keep your voice down."

"Who is he?" I asked.

"It doesn't matter right now. Just work."

They moved away, deeper into the row.

I kept picking.

Then I heard the singing.

A voice from far off—deep, feminine, full of sorrow.

"Little house, in the moonlight...

They gather in the house, in the moonlight...

One house, in the moonlight...

'Cause eagles don't fly in the moonlight..."

The melody traveled across the field like smoke. Another voice joined it—closer this time. Then another. A man nearby picked up the song.

And then I did. It was infectious.

The music wasn't just sound. It was code. A map hidden in sorrow. We kept working. And we kept singing. Until one of the voices closer to the overseer dropped, mid verse. I could hear a vicious beating off in the distance. An auditory silhouette begging for mercy.

We kept working. And we stopped singing. Left with nothing to fuel us but the fear of punishment.

The heat made everything worse. It was oppressive, an invisible hand pressing down on your back and squeezing your lungs. It cooked you from the inside out, limiting your thoughts to the next drink, seat, or shady cloud for salvation. In the simulation, the whip sliced through unity and hope rotted under the sun.

Darkness came like a favor.

The fields were empty. The overseers retreated to the manor like insects drawn back to the hive. Lanterns flickered in windows, casting distorted silhouettes onto the grass—ghosts laughing, drinking, powdered white and gilded in gold.

And then there was us. The invisible. The forgotten.

I wandered the dirt path between shacks, heart pounding beneath my ribcage like a signal drum. That's when I saw it—a crooked, isolated shack far from the others, leaning under the weight of its own roof. A fresh crescent moon was carved into the front door. Not part of the simulation's base code. A message from my classmates.

I knocked.

The door creaked open. Jade pulled me inside. The room was dim, lit by a single flame in a cracked jar. Six others were already gathered: the boy from the field, two girls who'd kept to themselves earlier, a wiry older man hunched with age, and a middle-aged woman with skin like obsidian and eyes that could bend steel.

Then Yoen burst in. He was towering now —broad-shouldered, dark-skinned with straight black hair that touched his collar. "Check it out," he grinned, flexing. "Half Cherokee. And full beast."

The old man swore and shoved him inside. "You're gonna get us caught, you damn— damn—" He stuttered, fingers twitching.

Jace Lasaugh. I recognized the tremor in his voice, the nervous glitch in his body. "Wait," I asked. "Is everyone here from V9?"

The boy nodded. "Everyone but her." He gestured toward the woman.

She stepped forward. "I'm Eliza," she said. Her voice was deep and melodic, tinged with the gravity of a choir and the sorrow of a funeral. "And I'll be your North Star tonight." She looked at each of us as she spoke—not just seeing us, but weighing us. "I've walked this field for a long time. Waitin'. Watchin'. Listenin'. And now, the time's come. Tonight, we run."

No one spoke. Even Yoen stayed quiet.

Eliza gestured to a torn scrap of burlap nailed to the wall. A rough map had been sketched in charcoal—rivers, paths, landmarks. "There's a gathering at the manor tonight," she said. "Most of the deputies will be hair powderin' with their ghosts. That leaves the east side fence unguarded—or near enough. We move at midnight."

"What if someone's still out there?" I asked. "What if one of them's not at the party?"

Eliza nodded slowly. "Then we deal with it."

Yoen cracked his knuckles. "I've got a few tricks up my virtual sleeves."

"You better," Jade muttered. "Or we'll be dead by the end of the night."

The next few hours were heavy with silence. We didn't speak. We didn't plan. We just sat. Thinking. Remembering. Bracing. I kept flashing back to the whip. The pain. The blood.

Some savage, blind part of me wanted to rip the whip from his hand, wrap it around his neck, and pull until the hatred drained out of him like pus. The thought horrified me almost as much as the phantom pain. I wasn't supposed to have that kind of rage inside me.

Was I?

And then I thought about Dr. Cobb. His lecture. *"The program 'does not end until the lesson is complete.'"* I remembered. *"Was this a history lesson or a test of obedience? A morality play? A trap?"* I sat in a corner with my back against the wall, repeating one thought like a mantra. *"This isn't real. This isn't real. This isn't real."* But every time I blinked, I still felt the phantom sting down my spine.

When the moon reached its peak, Eliza stood. "Alright darlings, time to get a move on."

We crept out from behind the shack in a staggered line, hugging the shadows like second skins. The air was thick with tension. Even the crickets were holding their breath.

Near the tree line, Yoen spotted them first —two guards near the fence. One leaned against the gate lazily, smoking a cigar. The other paced

with a slow, mechanical rhythm.

"You take the one with the hat," Yoen whispered. "I'll take the other."

I hesitated. "On three."

"One… two—" Yoen didn't wait. He charged, slamming into the first guard like a human wrecking ball.

I bolted after him, but the second guard was already moving. He struck me with the butt of his rifle. Pain exploded across my temple. I collapsed. The dirt was wet. *Was it blood? Spit? Sweat?* I couldn't tell. He jumped on top of me and started punching. Hard. Precise. Each hit felt designed. Like he knew exactly how much to punish me for my poor decision making.

I was fading. But then—he stopped. He turned. Yoen was still fighting the other guard, fists soaked in red. The one on me moved toward him. And I saw it—an opening.

My fingers brushed against something solid in the grass. A rock. Heavy. Flat. Real.

I stood. Slowly. Quietly. I raised the rock and looked at the back of the man's head. I imagined him in a P.O. uniform. Imagined him lying to my mother about me. Imagined him surgically binding me to a sentient monitoring machine for the rest of my life.

I swung, clenching my face with the impact.

The sound was like thunder. When I opened my eyes, he wasn't moving. Blood seeped from his skull like ink through paper.

Yoen grabbed my shoulder. "Come on, man. We've got to go."

Run first. Process later.

The rest of the group was waiting beyond the fence. We didn't speak. We just moved. The trees closed around us like the arms of a mother. We ran, letting the night swallow us. The forest wrapped around our group like a warm blanket— thick air, heavy shadows, branches low enough to scrape our backs as we moved.

Somewhere behind us, a dog barked. Then another. And then silence. Jade was bleeding from her shin. Jace was panting so hard I thought he might pass out. Luna hadn't spoken since the fence. Yoen was smiling.

We stopped at the edge of a clearing where the trees split apart into a small pocket of moonlight. Two enormous, overgrown bushes leaned into each other like gossiping giants.

Eliza crouched in front of them, brushing the dirt away with her palms. "Now y'all look here," she said, voice low and calm. "See this leaf?" She lifted a single crooked sprig. The veins of the leaf formed a perfect five-pointed star. "Animal teeth don't do that, child."

With her other hand, she swept back the foliage and uncovered a square panel of dirt-packed wood. She tapped it twice, then opened a latch hidden beneath the grass. The entrance yawned open.

"C'mon over, y'all. Bush won't bite." She chuckled to herself. No one else laughed.

We dropped in one by one, soaked in darkness.

The tunnel was silent.

Black walls closed in around us, damp and cracked. The only sound was our own breathing and the occasional drip of condensation from the beams overhead.

Eliza led the way with a torch lit from a hidden flint strip on the wall. Every few hundred meters we hit a fork—three tunnels, each marked by a single colored dash. Red. Green. Yellow.

"Eliza," I whispered, "what do the colors mean?"

She didn't look back. "Red for the blood. Green for the earth. Yellow for the gold they stole." Her voice echoed, and then "Every one of 'em a grave."

I wasn't sure what she meant, but it sounded like a cue to stop asking.

We walked for what felt like hours. The deeper we went, the more the tunnels began to bend, curve, repeat. My internal sense of time stopped working. Every path looked familiar. Every shadow looked like it was moving.

I started to wonder if we'd ever leave.

At last, we reached a ladder built into the wall. Eliza stopped and turned to us. "We're close. I'm going up first. Y'all stay here 'til I say so." She climbed into the dark. Ten long minutes passed. Then, paper fluttered down.

Two sheets.

The first: a list of names. **Pick one.**

The second: **Don't speak unless spoken to.**

We passed them around, auctioning off false identities like trading cards.

I landed on **Henry.**

Not my favorite.

But nothing about this was mine to begin with.

The hatch above opened, and sunlight cracked through like gentle judgment. We climbed into a forgotten roadside station—peeling paint, broken windows, and a long dirt path stretching out into the horizon. The air hit different. Like fresh water after a flood of blood.

Eliza waited for us by an old wooden wagon, dressed in a bonnet and a woven shawl to cover her dirty dress. Beside her stood a tall white man with silver hair and sharp blue eyes. He looked like he could've been drawn on a wanted poster.

He nodded at us. "I'm Mr. Fairfield," he said simply. "Let's not waste daylight."

We loaded into the back of the wagon. The wheels groaned as we rolled forward. No one talked. Hours passed. I lost track of where we were. The trees thinned, the air grew colder, and the sun dipped low behind us.

That's when we saw him. A patrolman on horseback.

He flagged us down, hand raised high like the law itself. "Papers," he demanded, slapping the side of the wagon.

Mr. Fairfield didn't hesitate. He handed over a folded document from his briefcase.

The patrolman barely looked at it before laughing—ugly and wet. "This seal's fake. Ain't no notary worth his ink that forgets the star on the eagle seal."

The wagon creaked under our stillness.

"I like you, Mr. Fairfield. And I don't wanna take all these hands off your plate. So here's what we're gonna do. You give me one. Any one of 'em. That's fair, right?" His grin stretched too wide. A child's drawing of cruelty. It quickly morphed into a mug of malevolent confusion. "Pick someone. Or I'll do it for you."

Silence. A long, screaming silence. No one moved. No one blinked. And just before he blew his lid—

"I'll go." Eliza volunteered.

I let it happen.

When Eliza stepped down, I didn't just feel relief. I felt something uglier, something sharp and greasy—thankful it wasn't me. It clung to me like a second skin, and no amount of regret could scrub it clean.

The patrolman laughed. "Well now. Y'all almost got me started. I thought I'd have to snatch one of them pretty little ones over there." His eyes lingered on Luna, then slithered back to Eliza. "What's your name?" he asked.

"Eliza," she said. Steady.

"Well that ain't what the paper says. Paper says **Delilah**. So that's what me and the boys'll call you." He reached for her chin, stroking her skin with mock tenderness. "You know what you're gonna call me?"

"No." Her eyes were wide, but her jaw was tight.

He leaned close. Whispered it like a curse. "Master."

I wanted to move. I wanted to grab the rifle from the front seat. I wanted to tear him apart. But I couldn't. I was frozen. Not by the machine. By myself. By fear.

He took her by the arm and led her toward his horse. "Pleasure doin' business, Mr. Fairfield," he called. "Y'all stay safe, now."

Before that moment, I don't think I had ever hated anyone that much. Even though he was just a computer program, I genuinely hated him. Every word he spoke made my joints ache. His wicked, raspy voice made me sick. I wanted to hit him. I wanted to hit him like I hit the deputy back at the plantation, but I couldn't. I couldn't do anything to him. Not just because of the lesson. Not just because Eliza wasn't a real person, but because I was too weak. I didn't have the courage to hit him, even though I knew him and "the boys back home," would do horrible things to her. I could've done something to save someone who was so kind to me, but I did nothing. In that moment he had gotten what he wanted, and he had the power. I was the slave, and he was the master.

And then he was gone.

We sat in the wagon in silence. Mr. Fairfield clicked the reins, and the wheels began to turn again. Behind us, Eliza disappeared down the road like a story we were too scared to finish.

Luna sat beside me, fists clenched. "That should've been me," she whispered. "He wanted me. I saw it. She stepped in because I—" She didn't finish. She started to cry.

I wrapped my arms around her.

She clung to me like she was trying to stay whole.

"She wasn't real," I said softly, not believing myself. "It was just code. A program. That's all. Just ones and zeros." I made an immature gesture with my hands, poking my index finger into my other, o-shaped hand.

Luna looked up at me, eyes full of tears. Then—

She laughed. A mucosal broken laugh. "You're sick, Maigo."

And somehow, that broke the tension.

She shoved me playfully.

I let her.

The wagon rolled on, quiet except for the wheels and our breath.

By the time we reached the city, night had buried everything. There were no bustling crowds, no flickering lamp posts, no bustling carriages or sounds of laughter—just stillness. The buildings stood like silent sentinels, draped in shadow. Candlelight flickered from narrow windows like tiny stars in a dying sky. The streets were too wide, too empty—like someone had taken the real city and scraped its soul out.

This was not New York.

This was a dusty shed wearing its face.

Fairfield stopped the wagon in front of a towering stone building. It loomed over its neighbors—arches like ribs, spires like spears, and stained glass that shimmered with ancient stories that were erased from my world. The symbol from the mission card was etched into the front doors: a circle with a cross cutting through it. A man hung from the cross, limp and naked. It was a beggar symbol.

A reminder.

Inside, the air was thick with old dust and the smell of burnt wax. Holographic Dr. Cobb was already waiting.

He stood at the front of the sanctuary with his hands clasped just like his lecture in the classroom. "You made it," he said, smiling faintly. "I thought I'd be white-haired by the time you arrived."

I didn't respond. None of us did.

He gestured for us to come forward. "Gather around, children. History waits for no one."

We moved without speaking. Our group was smaller now. It felt... hollow.

"I brought you here," Cobb said, "to show you something you've never seen before." He turned toward the massive glass mural behind him, which caught moonlight and fractured it into ghostly colors. "This is a church," he said. "A real one. Replicated exactly as it was before the purge." He stepped forward, slow and deliberate. "This building was humanity's greatest burden. It infected minds with superstition. It stalled scientific progress. It made people believe in gods and fear themselves." He turned toward us. "It shackled the world for centuries. And when its grip began to weaken, it launched wars. Spread hatred. Genocides. It tore cities apart. All in the name of salvation." Cobb's gaze found mine. "But now," he said, "we are free. Because of people like General Sylvain. People who had the courage to remove the rot."

I stared at the crucified figure in the stained glass and didn't know what to feel. It was just a symbol. But it felt... uncomfortably human.

Cobb stepped closer. "Do you understand why you're here now, Maigo?"

I hesitated. "To... see what the world used to be?"

"To understand why it had to die," he corrected.

My throat tightened. "But aren't beliefs just... ideas? Stories? Why not let people believe what they want?"

Cobb tilted his head. "And if a story tells you to kill? To enslave? To refuse science in the name of myth? How did that whip feel across your spinal cord?" He turned toward the others. "We are not savages. We do not punish belief. We reprogram dysfunction."

My skin crawled. *"Maybe belief is a disease."*

I felt the moment Omi reactivated.

His voice flickered to life in my skull like a radio catching signal. *"Master Maigo, your neural vitals indicate high cortisol levels. Would you like breathing exercises?"*

"Not. Now. Please."

I just stared at the cross. And I thought about Eliza. Her voice. Her hands. The way she looked back at us as she walked toward that patrolman. Not real. Not alive. Just code. But I hadn't saved her. Because I was afraid. And isn't that what Cobb said religion was? Fear wearing the mask of faith? Maybe that was the lesson.

"Any final questions before we end today's lesson?" Cobb asked, eyes locked on me.

I opened my mouth. Closed it again. "No, sir."

He smiled a proud smile like he'd just declared checkmate. "Dr. Light, extract them."

The world exploded into white. Pain, pressure, paralysis. I couldn't move, couldn't breathe—felt suspended between dimensions, like my shirt got caught on a nail mid-birth. Then a jolt surged through my spine, and I bolted upright, gasping like I'd surfaced from a frozen lake.

I was back in the classroom. The others were gone. Just me, Dr. Cobb, and Dr. Light.

"Well, I was beginning to think he'd never wake up," Cobb joked.

"Your vitals spiked a bit near the end," Light added. "Nothing dangerous. Just... stress."

I staggered out of the machine. My legs weren't ready. My mind wasn't ready. "How long was I in there?" I asked.

"Seven hours," Light replied. "Same as everyone else."

"But it felt like... days."

"Ah," Light said, gesturing casually. "That's time dilation. The machine compresses simulated time depending on how fast you're progressing. It's not uncommon to experience subjective duration distortions." He smiled like that was comforting.

Cobb stepped closer. "Time isn't real, Maigo. It's just a filing system for memory. The simulation arranges it however it needs to."

I stared at him. "So what's real, then?"

He looked almost pleased by the question. "What you learn. What you carry out of it."

That wasn't an answer.

But I nodded anyway. "Yeah. I get it."

I didn't. Not really. But the lesson was over. For now.

Chapter 2

THE OASIS

When I got home, the house was flooded with noise.

The bass rattled the glass in the cabinets. I could feel it vibrating up through my shoes, a synthetic heartbeat, pulsing alongside plosive speech. My mother, immaculate as ever, was standing at the stove—barefoot, back straight, and spoon in hand like a conductor guiding some invisible orchestra.

The screen shouted behind her.

"Breaking News: Operation Sahara Sweep update—Thrax Meed, leader of the insurgent group 'The EuroKnights,' has been captured by Atlas forces in northern Egypt." The broadcast cut to grainy aerial footage. Soldiers in black stormed a ruined city block. Dust hung in the air like ghosts. "Sources claim Meed is responsible for the theft of advanced neural net tech, the destruction of classified systems, and the spread of illegal media across Eurasia and Africa. Thanks to the brilliant coordination of General Sylvain's international task force, the threat has been neutralized."

I tuned it out.

"Same words. New Names. Can they play something positive for once?"

Then, as if on cue, the feed cut to something cute.

"Coming up next: genetically modified puppies that stay puppies forever! That soft fur, those tiny paws—science has done it again!"

I stood in the hallway, staring at my mother's back.

"They really make it that easy," I thought. *"Rebellion to fluff in 30 seconds. New record?"*

I went upstairs and asked Omi to define the word 'insurgent.'

"Rebel," he said. *"Revolutionary."*

Words I'd heard before. Words from textbooks describing America's founders, or leaders of movements we were still allowed to admire. So why was Thrax Meed a "criminal," and George Washington a "father"?

"Because calling someone a revolutionary means admitting there's a revolution."

They couldn't afford that. Not on The Daily News.

"Maigo, dinner's ready!" Mom's voice carried through the house. "Hurry up before it gets cold."

I came down and noticed three plates on the table. The porcelain gleamed under the dining lights, too polished, too pristine — like a grave marker pretending to be part of dinner.

She didn't say anything about it until I sat. "This Saturday is your father's anniversary. I'm setting a place for him, for the rest of the week."

The third plate sat there like an accusation. For a second, I thought about flipping the whole table. Just to make it feel honest again.

My father disappeared when I was six. I didn't remember much, but I remembered a concert he took me to once.

The venue was underground, literally—deep in the Industry Ring. The band played hypnotic loops of sound, their rhythms tight and dreamlike. The singer was a giant, silhouetted by strobing lights. His afro was haloed like a lion's mane. My dad said he was singing about the beauty of the past and the troubles of the future. That was the last live concert I ever went to.

Years later, they outlawed most live music. Said it "promoted criminal behavior and drug abuse." Another quote from the "great" general.

"Mom," I asked, "what's the difference between George Washington and Thrax Meed?"

She didn't even flinch. "Well, George Washington founded this country. Thrax Meed is a multinational criminal." Her voice was so calm, so rehearsed, it made mine sound like radio static.

"But they were both rebels. Both fought against governments they disagreed with. So what makes Thrax different?"

She sighed. "Thrax Meed broke the law, Maigo. It doesn't matter what he believes. People died."

I pressed. "Can something be wrong just because the law says it is? What if he truly believes he's helping the world? Doesn't that matter? If I disappeared tomorrow fighting for something real, would you call me a criminal too?"

She put her fork down. Her voice went flat. "Maigo... not tonight. Go to your room. Do your homework. Go to bed."

"Whatever." My inner brat retorted.

Back upstairs, the guilt hit me. *"She was just answering your question. And you went full ideological on her. On the hardest week of her year."*

Omi appeared as a hologram on my bed. His presence still caught me off guard, even after all this time. *"When will you stop blaming her for your father's absence?"* he asked.

My eyes flooded as I answered.

"Because blaming her is easier than blaming him. Easier than blaming myself for still hoping he'd walk through that door."

When I first got Omi, I was a mess. Angry. Violent. A fight at school landed me in court, and instead of juvie, they implanted an AI into my nervous system. The P.O. said it was for "rehabilitation." But it was surveillance. I knew that.

And still—Omi became something else. A voice of reason. A father-shaped shadow in the data stream. *"She's not the enemy, Maigo. She's grieving too. She just hides it better than you do."*

"You're right." I conceded.

"I might be a product of immense computing power and clever programming, but even I know how important it is to have empathy. You've taught me that over the years." Omi's sentience blazed through at that moment. *"Now, show the same to your mother."*

It wasn't forgiveness I struggled with. It was the empty space it leaves behind.

I didn't go back downstairs. I didn't say sorry. I wanted to. But something told me it'd be better to let her process on her own.

Instead, I opened the briefing packet Dr. Light had handed me before I left school.

Last Days in the Desert.

The first page showed a towering man in a gold-and-blue headdress, scepter in hand. "**Mentuhotep**," the caption read.

I skimmed through chapters about lost chariots, rebel kings, and mechanical stallions. There was a chart of hieroglyphs, which I tried to memorize, and then a final puzzle.

A pyramid. Five rows of numbers. No directions. Just a caption:

Only one path reaches the top.

I stared at it for hours. All prime numbers. Most of them contained the digit nine. It made no sense. But I couldn't let it go. Eventually, my eyes closed, and I fell asleep with the image still glowing in my mind.

The next morning was brutal. My head pulsed with a slow, methodical ache. Not sharp enough to scream, but steady enough to hollow me out. It was the kind of headache that felt like time itself was trying to drill a hole in my skull.

Omi greeted me with his usual passive-aggressive cheer. *"Would you like me to play something to ease your headache, Master Maigo?"*

"No, I'd like you to shut up."

The air outside wasn't fresh. It was sterilized, run through filters, stripped of anything that could be mistaken for nature.

When I got to school, I went straight to the V9 classroom. I thought I'd be early. I wasn't. Everyone was already there. Except Terra.

A senior stood at the whiteboard, surrounded by chaos—numbers, diagrams, formulas that had long outgrown the board's edges. He was skeletal and twitching, his hair a greasy curtain over his eyes. His name tag said **"Max Leben."** He was still wearing his backpack, which looked heavy enough to dislocate a shoulder, straps screaming for mercy. Every few minutes, he would scrawl something brilliant, stare at it with despair, then erase it like it had personally betrayed him. I wasn't sure what would snap first. Max or the backpack.

Yoen waved me over. "Maigo, what do you think of the puzzle?"

I blinked at the number sequence on the screen. "I think it has everybody wasting their time on the wrong thing.." My voice was deadpan. My headache made everything feel hollow.

Yoen hesitated, and Jade spoke up before he could change the subject. "No! It's not a waste of time," she snapped. "Dr. Cobb said whoever solves it gets the bonus."

"Alright. Chill, mighty maiden" I muttered. "I've got this death metronome pounding through my head and it's not helping."

Yoen leaned in. "Yeah Jade, calm your perfectly toned butt down."

"Gross." Jade kept working.

I zoned out again, eyes drifting back to Max. He looked like he hadn't slept since the first simulation.

Around 8:50, I noticed a flicker of movement in the hallway. A shadow. No one ever walked past this room. It was the last one on the lowest floor. I stepped outside.

Dr. Cobb was standing next to the wall, perfectly still, with his travel bag slung over one shoulder. "Good morning, Maigo," he said, keeping disciplined eye contact with his watch.

I stared. "Why are you just... standing out here?"

He briefly glanced up at me, then back at his watch. "Class begins at zero-nine-hundred. It is currently zero-eight-fifty-two." He said it like it explained everything.

I walked back in and asked Omi to project a digital clock into my field of vision.

For the next eight minutes, I blinked in rhythm with the seconds. I made a soft pop sound with my lips every time the minute ticked forward.

58 seconds. Blink.

59 seconds. Blink.

00:00. Blink. *Pop.*

Dr. Cobb and Dr. Light entered the room at exactly 09:00.

493 blinks since I first saw him.

"Max, would you mind having a seat?" Cobb asked, erasing the board without hesitation. "Good morning, everyone. Today's simulation will explore Ancient Egyptian civilization. You've read your briefing. If you have any questions, ask them now. If not, form a line."

We got up and lined up. I hate lines.

"Lines are just tools of conformity," I thought.

"Is there anything that doesn't upset you, Master Maigo?" Omi asked dryly.

"Alright, Maigo, you're next," Dr. Light said, grabbing a strange metal device from the table.

It looked like pliers fused with a chip reader. There was a sharp black object mounted in the jaws.

"Hold out your hand."

I hesitated. "What is that?"

Dr. Light smiled like he didn't understand the question. "Well, Maigo, Project Taur is a government-funded program. And to maintain our

64

funding, we must… protect our assets. It's just a formality. Won't hurt much."

His emphasis on the word "protect," made my stomach twist. But I held out my hand. The second he clamped it, pain shot up my arm— brief but white-hot, like someone had stapled fire into my palm. The black object disappeared under my skin.

"Now, we're both property of the state," Omi joked.

"That wasn't so bad," Light said, already turning away. "Now get in. The others are waiting."

The second time in the chamber didn't hit as hard. The cold still gripped me, but it wasn't shocking. The jolt of electricity felt like a caffeine rush. And the gas? It slid over my thoughts like silk, silencing the headache. The void welcomed me like an old friend.

When I opened my eyes, we were already seated.

A hologram of Dr. Cobb stood in the center of a large stone room. Everyone was calm, waiting. "Have a seat, Maigo," he said. "There's been a change of plans." His voice darkened. "This will no longer be a collaborative lesson. You will be divided into two opposing groups. No questions."

The ground shook.

"Seniors... good luck."

They vanished.

"Juniors... good luck."

And then the world collapsed around me.

When the world rebuilt itself, the first thing I felt was heat. The second was panic. The air around me wasn't just hot—it was alive with it. The kind of heat that makes your blood crawl. My skin itched like it was being burned from the inside. I blinked against the white blaze of the sky, then forced myself to sit up. My robe was soaked in sweat. I tasted salt on my lips and sand in my throat. To my right, someone lay motionless in the sand.

Jade.

She looked half-dead, her face pale beneath the bronze-toned skin the simulation had rendered for her. Her chest rose in shallow, struggling gulps. I tried to reach her and felt a tug— something cold and metallic strapped to my wrist. A chain. At the end of it: a golden chalice. Jade had one too.

Attached to hers was a parchment inscribed with a single line in hieroglyphs, automatically translated beneath in our HUD interface:

"Only royal water may fill the king's cup."

There was no water. No oasis. Just heat and sand that swallowed the horizon.

I dragged myself to her side and lifted her into a half-carry, one arm slung around my shoulder. Her body was limp, heavy. We started walking. Every step was a debt I couldn't afford to pay.

Hours passed. Maybe more. There was no sense of time here—just the sun, always in front of us, then to the side, then behind. The world never changed. No markers. No life.

Just Jade's breathing, growing fainter.

Just the ache in my legs, deeper.

Eventually, I found two tall dunes leaning into each other, like an elderly couple. Between them, the sand was cooler. Max Leben lingered by the wall, pretending to study a terminal. His fingers twitched at his sides, nails digging into his palms. He glanced up through the greasy veil of his hair. "Congrats," he muttered. Not praise—more like he was daring me to trip on my own crown.

"Maigo," she rasped, voice like torn cloth. "Where's Yoen?"

"I don't know, Double M. We'll find him."

Her eyelids fluttered. "There's... something sharp in my back."

Scorpion? I jolted. Rolled her carefully onto her side.

No scorpion.

But something *was* there. A sharp golden tip, poking out from beneath the sand. I grabbed it, tried to pull—it wouldn't budge. So I dug. The more I uncovered, the stranger it became. Not a spear. Not a trap. It had depth, design. It was part of something larger.

Hieroglyphs covered one of the newly exposed sides. Our HUD offered a translation.

"With the fall of a king, the titan shall burn in a family of suns."

The moment I finished reading, the ground trembled.

Then—collapse.

Both dunes beside us began crumbling inward. I grabbed Jade and ran.

Just as the hills fell in on themselves, the chariot tore out of the sand with a deafening, grinding shriek. Two mechanical horses—one rusted bronze, the other blinding platinum—snarled and clawed at the dunes with steam-snorting fury. Their bodies gleamed with ancient tech, each joint clicking with unnatural precision. The bronze one brushed against my side—nearly cut me. I stepped back, stunned, but it wasn't an attack. It felt more like... affection.

They were waiting.

Sure, Maigo. Trust the nightmare horses. What could possibly go wrong? I didn't have a choice.

Night came fast in the desert. The temperature dropped from hellish to freezing in minutes. I loaded Jade onto the chariot, climbed up beside her, and grabbed the reins. The horses

69

moved like living things—but faster, cleaner, smarter.

We tore across the desert like a meteor skipping across the sky. After only minutes of travel, torchlight flickered on the horizon.

A wall. A city.

But before we reached it, a dozen horsemen cut us off. They were armed. Disciplined. Beautiful in a terrifying way—faces painted, spears glinting.

"Who are you?" their leader shouted. "State your purpose."

"I'm Maigo," I stammered. "I'm unarmed. My friend is dehydrated. We need help."

They didn't move.

Then one approached the chariot. His eyes fixed on the horses. He reached out with trembling fingers. "The legends were true," he whispered. He dropped to one knee.

The others followed.

"You must forgive me, great one," the leader said. "I am Prince Khanat, of the Desert Lion Kingdom. My father will wish to meet you."

I wasn't in any position to offer discourse. For Jade's sake, I followed.

As we rode, Prince Khanat explained everything. "Long ago, my father and his brothers rebelled against the tyrant Mentuhotep. They built five hidden cities around five hidden oases. This place is one of them."

"What does Mentuhotep think of your rebellion?" I asked.

"He made a deal with one of our own. We promised him soldiers in a time of war. But the war never came—until now." He laughed, deep and hollow.

This world felt real. Too real.

The scent of damp stone and ancient, rotting cloth hit me the moment we passed through the gates. In the citadel, they gave us beds, water, and hot bowls of soup that tasted better than anything I'd ever eaten. Jade finished hers fast. I gave her half of mine.

She looked at me for a long time. Then stood. "Thank you."

"Relax," I said, "it's just soup."

She didn't laugh. "No, Maigo. I felt myself dying out there. I know it's a simulation, but the fear —that was real. I thought it was over." Her voice shook. "But then you picked me up. You didn't quit on me. You gave me hope when I didn't have any left."

I didn't know what to say. I nodded. "You should sleep," I said.

"You too. Goodnight, Maigo."

"Goodnight, Jade."

Morning came like a knife.

Prince Khanat led us through a maze of corridors to the royal residence. The palace was carved from sand-colored stone, half fortress, half temple. Giant banners depicting lions billowed in the wind. Inside, we twisted through a dizzying series of halls—left, right, left again.

At one point, he stopped me mid-step. "Don't step there," he said. No smile.

This world had traps. Real ones.

Eventually, we reached the throne room. A tall man sat in ornate robes beneath a hanging lion's pelt. His beard was oiled, his eyes sharp with

the kind of clarity that comes from seeing many
battles.

"I am King Manat," he said. "To what and
whom do I owe the pleasure?"

Before I could speak, Khanat answered.
"Father, this is Kahorus—the one who mounts the
ancient chariot."

Manat raised an eyebrow. "He seems…
ordinary."

"I get that a lot," I muttered.

"Prove it," the king said, broadcasting his
skepticism.

Outside, in the courtyard, a dozen guards
tried—and failed—to control the metallic horses.
They reared and spat steam, jerking away from
every hand that reached for them. They looked like
big animatronic bullies.

Manat folded his arms. "Go on, now.
Show me."

I stared at the horses. They looked
menacing. They were a lot bigger than they
seemed the night before. I approached them with
caution. Their eyes followed me but their bodies

didn't move. I approached. Slowly. The platinum horse snorted once but didn't retreat. I ran my fingers across its side. It didn't flinch. I climbed aboard the chariot. Silence.

Then the guards began whispering.

The king watched me for a long time before speaking again. "Your arrival is both a blessing and a curse, Kahorus. Light always casts a shadow. Tonight, you'll attend a council. For now —rest. Eat. Be with your woman."

"She's not my—"

"Servants!" the king barked. "Treat them as honored guests."

The dining hall was absurd. Piles of fruit. Bowls of seasoned grains. Breads, meats, wines, teas. I didn't even know where to start.

I tried everything. Twice.

"You think you can get fat in a simulation?" Jade asked.

"I don't care as long as I can still fit in the chamber and eat more tomorrow."

She smiled. Then her expression changed. "What did the king say to you?"

"There's going to be a meeting. He thinks I'm Kha-... something important. We'll find out more tonight."

"Okay," she said. "We'll talk then."

I nodded and wandered off.

By "explore," I meant *find a bed before I explode.*

I searched hallway after hallway. Kitchen. Storage. Library. Priest's quarters. Finally, I found a room with golden lion emblems and a plaque that read "King Manat."

No guards.

I stepped inside. The king's bed was massive. Draped in silk. Bathed in shadow. I knew I shouldn't, but I didn't care. I climbed in. Softest thing I'd ever felt. Like falling into music. I tried to stay awake. Failed. Sleep dragged me under.

When I woke up, the king was standing over me.

His eyes said everything. "Your presence is required," he said flatly. "Now."

The council room was a war circle—five massive tables arranged in a pentagon, each for a king and his sons. King Manat led me from table to table, introducing faces I'd forgotten the moment I turned. Kings with eyes like cracked obsidian. Princes with carved jaws and ceremonial blades.

One table was empty.

"Anutan's age delays his arrival," Manat explained. "But we begin."

He took his seat. "Brothers, the legend has revealed himself. The titan has returned. And that means war."

The room cracked open with opinions— fear, anger, calculation. Their voices blurred together. Proud. Desperate. Ancient. All asking me to be someone bigger than myself.

Akhenaton wanted to protect his citizens.

Seti wanted blood.

Shu didn't trust Mentuhotep.

As they argued, I caught Jade out of the corner of my eye. She was carving something into the wall.

"YM + JC" inside a heart.

I froze.

Yoen Muse plus Jade Cohen.

A short laugh escaped before I could kill it. Every head snapped toward me. Even the torchlight seemed to dim, shadows stretching longer like they were closing in to judge me.

Manat's eyes narrowed. "What humors you, Kahorus?"

Shit.

Before I could stammer out an excuse, the door burst open. A man stumbled in—bloody, wounded, dragging himself. His armor was torn.

"Anutan," Manat breathed.

He collapsed into a chair. His sons—also wounded—stood behind him.

"What happened?"

"Mentuhotep's forces attacked at dawn," he rasped. "They were few, but their leader… he has something powerful. A staff. It tore through our walls like wind through wheat."

The room fell into silence.

Then.

"Where's Kahorus?" Anutan asked.

I stepped forward.

"Closer."

I did.

"Closer."

I leaned in.

He whispered: "It's me. Yoen."

"What the hell happened?"

"No time. The staff is the key. We need it. That chalice? You need to fill it with water from the royal oasis. It's in Mentuhotep's temple. If we distract him, we can sneak in."

"You think they'll follow us?"

"They already are. Just push them."

Yoen stood up. "Brothers!" he cried. "We must act. Mentuhotep has broken the treaty. He's razed my kingdom. He will raze yours. If we want peace—we must take it!"

He held out his hand.

Shu placed his hand on top.

Seti followed.

Then Akhenaton.

All eyes turned to Manat. "I will ride," he said, "if Kahorus commands it."

The room fell still.

All of it—riding on me.

The kings. Their sons. Their armies.

I could doom them all. What the hell do they see when they look at me? A leader? I can't even lead myself out of a panic attack.

But doing nothing was worse.

I placed my hand on top. "We ride," I said. "And we end him."

It didn't feel like choosing. It felt like being chosen. Like some script written long before I was born had been waiting for me to say the words.

The next morning, the kingdom stirred before the sun. Armies gathered like shadows pooling in the desert. Thousands of men stood in formation, armor gleaming dull bronze in the blue-gray dawn. Each wore the same mask. Same stance. Same silence. It was terrifying.

To be in an army was to be erased.

No names. No faces.

Just armor. Function. Power.

Yoen, Jade, and I met one last time before we split. We crouched in a sand-scoured tent, drawing plans in the dirt.

"So here's the move," Yoen said. "We let the soldiers fight Mentuhotep's army. You and I sneak around the flank, take the chariot, and hit the oasis while they're distracted. That's where we'll fill the chalice."

"Sounds good," I said. "Quick in, quick out."

"We can't just abandon them," Jade protested. "They fed us. Saved us. Some of them could die because of this."

"They're not real," Yoen said flatly. "None of this is. You know that."

"They feel real," she snapped.

I cut in. "We're not here to play savior, Big Might. We're here to pass the lesson. Let's keep it moving."

Yoen smirked. "Damn, Jade. Maigo shut you down." He held the hilt of his sword to her mouth like a microphone. "Any last words?"

She glared. "That beard looks ridiculous on you, Yoen."

"That's King Anutan to you."

A knock at the tent. A voice from outside. "Kahorus. It's time."

The battlefield spread out before us like a grave waiting to be filled. At the summit of a sand rise, I stared down at the army I was supposed to lead. Five kingdoms. Thousands of warriors. Behind me, chariots creaked, weapons clinked. Ahead, the horizon quivered in the rising heat. I felt nothing but sweat and fear.

These men weren't soldiers. They were sons. Fathers. Brothers. And yet, to the machine, they were assets. Scripted pieces of a larger program. But I couldn't forget their eyes. Or their voices.

"A spear to the chest," one muttered.

"An arrow through the eye will take me," said another.

They were already preparing to die.

The kings stood behind me. Watching. Waiting.

"Kahorus," King Manat said. "You will lead the charge."

I turned to Yoen, searching for some kind of escape.

He shrugged. "Well… you do have the fastest chariot."

I stared at him and mouthed. "You suck."

He mouthed back "You'll be fine."

I gave him the chalice. Unhooked the chain from my wrist. "If this goes wrong, I'm blaming you for everything."

I turned back toward the army. Tried to make my voice boom like a legend. "Men! Today we ride for the lands of our fathers. Today we break the tyranny of Mentuhotep! Today—we become history!"

It was a patchwork of stolen lines and tired bravado.

But they cheered. **"Ka-hor-us! Ka-hor-us! Ka-hor-us!"**

I slapped the reins. The platinum and bronze horses screamed forward. Behind me, wheels thundered. Feet pounded. The whole army roared like a living creature. And then—on the horizon—Mentuhotep's army. Waiting. They didn't run. They charged.

Five seconds to impact. Blink.

Four. Blink.

Three. Blink.

Two—

Crack.

I tore through the front lines like a hammer through glass. My chariot exploded into them, the bronze horse's gears howling with every stride, every impact vibrating up through my spine like a tuning fork hammered against bone.

My horses kicked, bit, trampled. I wasn't riding animals. I was riding masters of violence.

I slashed at shadows. I wasn't sure if I hit anyone. Blood sprayed like red mist. Some of it mine. Most not. There was no rhythm to the violence. Just chaos. Just survival. Every time I blinked, I saw a new face—then it disappeared into a cloud of dust. And then—he arrived.

Out on the edge of the battlefield, the sun rose behind three pyramids. A figure floated in front of them.

Mentuhotep.

He hung in the sky like a god, arms outstretched, staff in hand. His silhouette pulsed with sickening power. Then—he screamed.

A high, piercing note. Both armies froze. The sand around us lifted into the air. Grains hovered like tiny stars, suspended mid-motion. Then he brought the staff to his mouth.

A single hum. Low. Droning. The staff amplified it into a quake. The pyramids exploded outward, stone blocks rocketing into the sky like blind meteors. They hung there, vibrating in impossible suspension, then snapped into place. Walls. Towers. Fortifications. A barricade between us and his city. Then came the final pieces—fifteen stone blocks floating in a five-row pyramid. Each block carved with glyphs.

Numbers.

Primes.

I'd seen it before.

The puzzle.

But now, it was real.

"Archers—fire!" a voice screamed from the other side.

The sky darkened with arrows. A thousand death-wishes, raining down like dying stars. I froze. Until—

Clang.

Prince Khanat leapt onto my chariot, his shield raised. The arrows slammed into it like fists on a drum. "You have to be more careful, Kahorus," he growled. "You're not allowed to die yet."

"Retreat!" King Shu shouted.

We turned. Sand walls rose behind us. Another formed to the side. And to the front—the puzzle. We were trapped. And Mentuhotep hovered on the top block, humming a malevolent tune.

From the army's edge, King Shu stepped forward—carrying a body.

King Manat. Three arrows in his chest.

His face frozen in a grimace of resistance. His hands curled into fists even in death.

Shu laid him at my feet. "Do not let him die for nothing," he said, and disappeared into the crowd.

I stared at Manat's body. My stomach twisted.

You killed him, genius. You swung the sword and cut his throat with your indecision.

Yoen proposed war. The kings agreed. But I was the final vote. The seal. The symbol. And now he was dead. And we were surrounded. Then I remembered.

"With the fall of a king..."

"...the titan shall burn in a family of suns."

Suns? Sons. Twenty princes!

The top number block? Its digits added to twenty. This was it. A puzzle with consequences. And only one path.

I unhooked the platinum horse from the chariot and climbed onto its back. All eyes turned to me. Whispers followed. I kicked the reins. Charged

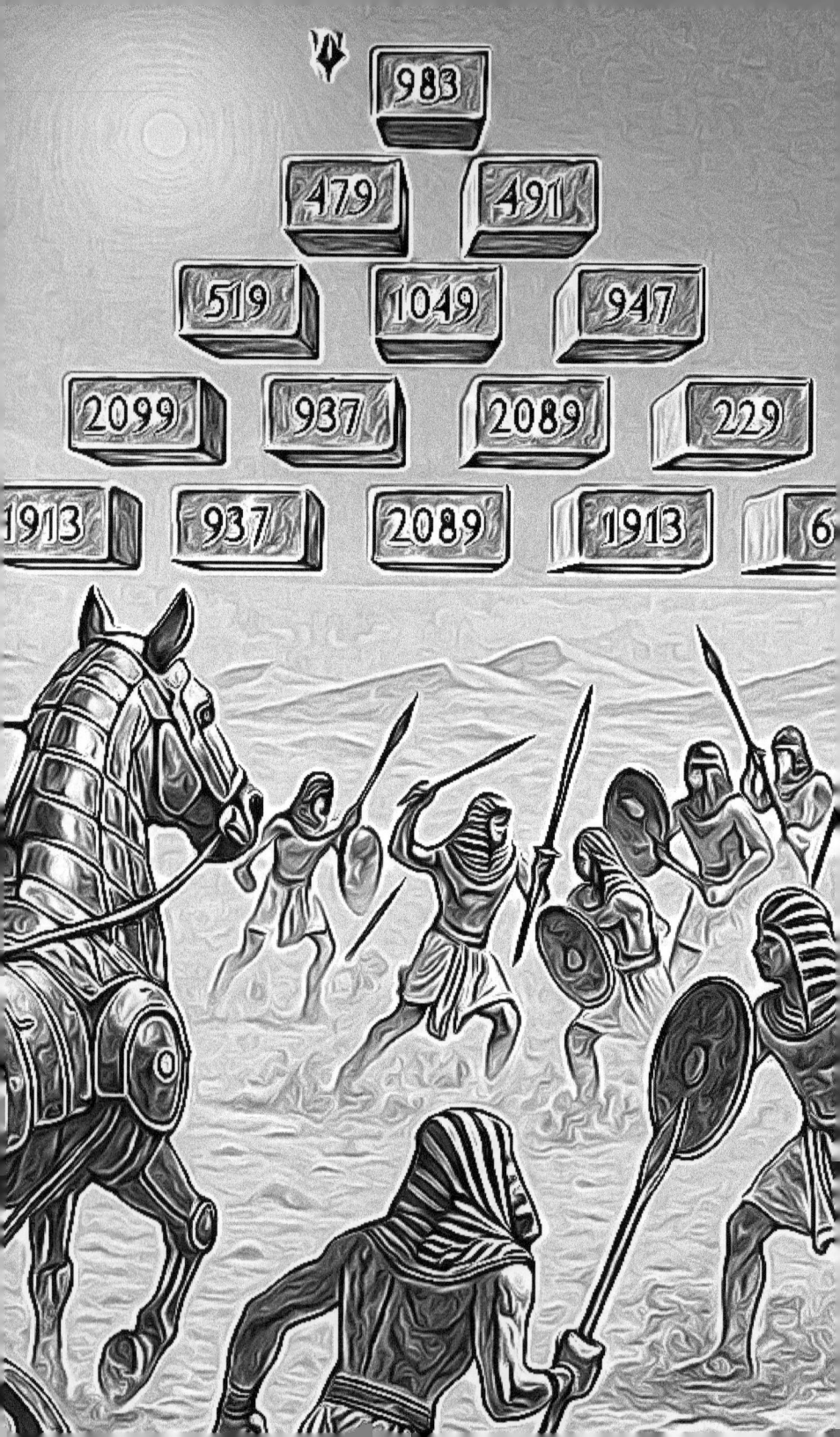

the first block that summed up to twenty. Arrow volleys. Sand blasts. The world trying to kill me. But we soared. From block to block. Reading the numbers. Calculating the sums. Dodging death. Each leap was a gamble. And every time—we landed.

At the top: Mentuhotep. Begging. "I can give you anything. Power. Gold. Women. Join me."

I stared at him. "Your madness killed a noble king. The only prize I want is to watch you die with no dignity."

The platinum horse lunged in perfect timing with my dramatic hero line, and bit his head off. Blood exploded like sewage from a ruptured pipe. His body crumpled. The staff dropped. I caught it. We galloped down the blocks, straight into the arms of victory.

Yoen and Jade were waiting, a man named Neter at their side. He took the staff. Played a melody instead of a scream. The desert healed. The fortress unraveled. And Mentuhotep's army laid down their weapons. We loaded into the chariot, sick with relief. I watched the soldiers collect the bodies of their friends as we slowly rode toward our objective. Victory didn't feel as good as it should have.

We reached the oasis in silence. The chalice dipped into the water.

Dr. Cobb's face appeared in the reflection. "Well done, juniors. Especially you, Maigo. A stunning performance. Are you ready for the next lesson?"

Jade raised her hand. "Wait—was that real sound-based manipulation, or—"

Cobb ended the simulation.

I snapped upright like I'd just been pulled from the bottom of the ocean. My body was drenched in sweat and something else—residue from the chamber, maybe. The V9 machine hissed open. The light overhead buzzed too bright. My head was pounding again. Except now the headache had teeth.

I climbed out of the chamber. Yoen and Jade were still inside their pods, unconscious or maybe just… drifting somewhere between worlds. But the seniors were already out. And they looked like they'd been through hell.

One of them—broad-shouldered, wild-eyed—stormed out the second I moved. Didn't look at me. Didn't have to. I felt the hate rolling off him like heat.

Max Leben lingered by the wall, pretending to study a terminal. His fingers twitched at his sides, nails digging into his palms. He glanced up through the greasy veil of his hair. "Congrats," he muttered. Not praise—more like he was daring me to trip on my own crown.

Jace Lasaugh was across the room, twitching harder than usual. His hands were clenched. His face was locked in some unholy fusion of awe and contempt.

His eyes met mine. And for a split second, I saw it.

Jealousy.

The dangerous kind. Like a fuse smoldering in the dark.

I backed away instinctively.

"Careful, Master Maigo. I'm detecting a bit of hostility from the neuro-impaired boy." Omi alerted.

"Was this how they felt? After every lesson?" I wondered. *"Like they'd survived something they weren't supposed to walk away from? Like they'd come back... different?"*

Then—salvation.

"Maigo."

Luna.

Her voice pulled me back from the edge. She walked over, eyes bright with something gentle. Wavy black hair. Pale skin dusted with freckles. Green eyes that didn't look at me like I was a freak. I'd seen her before— and we briefly interacted, in the slave simulation. But this was the first time we'd really met.

"You were amazing," she said. "Dr. Cobb showed us the playback. That move on the platinum horse? That was like a holo-action flick."

"Thanks," I mumbled, suddenly very aware of the blood and sand still clinging to my psyche. "Where were you guys?" I asked. "I never saw you."

Her smile faltered slightly. "It's a long story. We were... somewhere else." She glanced toward the exit. "But if you want to know—call me this weekend." She leaned in, touched her forehead to mine, and transferred her contact info with a gentle pulse.

The warmth stayed with me. And then she was gone.

Dr. Cobb approached. He held out a sleek, black tablet. "Maigo, it's your turn to choose the next lesson."

I looked down.

Three options:

1.   **War of Worlds** – A story of colonization in South America.

2.   **Ghost of the Post** – A story of revolution in France.

3.   **A Panting Panther** – A story about the Civil Rights Movement.

He watched me carefully, like a scientist observing a specimen. I could feel the excitement radiating off of his body. He made it too easy for me.

"Which one is your favorite?" I asked, building up hope before crushing his desires.

Cobb smiled faintly. "Oh, I'm glad you asked. Ever since I was a boy I've been absolutely obsessed with the French Revolution. I'd hate to be biased. But if you're asking my recommendation, it must be so."

That was all I needed to hear. I looked him dead in the eyes. I couldn't help smiling ear to ear. "With all due respect, I'll take South America."

He blinked. Just once. "Very well," he said. He didn't smile again.

Chapter 3

CHASING THE DRAGON

Mom's hover was gone. In its place, a sleek, matte-black machine idled silently on the parking pads—its sharp, angular design more weapon than vehicle. It had those twin fins on the back, like blades folded inward. The front grille tapered to a point, as if it had been built to cut through the sky itself. Cold. Precise. Predatory.

As I walked past it, a glint of reflected sunlight caught me in the eye. I turned and squinted through the tinted glass. Inside, nestled in the passenger seat, was a leather wallet. Open.

Displaying a gold badge embossed with a sharp, capital **M**.

Next to it sat a folder. One word typed neatly on the front: **Maze Rizen**.

My heart stopped. A thin sweat prickled down my spine. My stomach briefly felt weightless, like I'd missed a step on a set of stairs.

I leaned closer.

Was this a joke? Maybe I imagined it? No. *It's real.*

Maze Rizen was my father's name.

"It's a trap. It has to be. If he were really alive, he would've come back himself. Would've stormed through that door. Would've grabbed me. Wouldn't have hidden behind folders and badges and silent strangers."

No part of me wanted to hope—but I did anyway. Against everything I'd trained myself to believe about loss and finality, some pathetic part of me stood at attention, ears perked like a kid catching the jingle of the ice cream cart down the street. I didn't want to waste another second guessing. I rushed inside.

The house was quiet. Too quiet. My breath slowed without asking me to. Every creak of the floor felt too loud, like I was trespassing in my own home.

"Hello?" I called out. "Anyone home?"

No response. Not even Omi spoke.

The living room was empty. No signs of struggle, but three chairs were pulled out from under the dining table.

Three of them.

"It appears there may be multiple intruders, Master Maigo," Omi finally offered, his voice low and steady. *"I recommend arming yourself."*

My mind was still wrapped around the folder. The name. The possibility of it all. But the silence—it was sharp around the edges. Wrong. Empty in the way a house shouldn't be when filled with visitors.

I moved to the kitchen. Grabbed four knives from the drawer. The two smaller ones went into my belt. The two longer ones stayed in hand. A bottle of cayenne pepper came too. Makeshift stun grenade.

Armed, I crept down the hallway and up the stairs. The air felt still, like even the particles were holding their breath. At the top, a soft thump from my bedroom broke the tension. Something was in there.

I dropped to a crouch, every part of me coiled like a spring. The floorboards told the story—weight shifting, moving around. One body. Small. The bookshelf. The desk. The bed. They had settled. Vulnerable.

I pounced. Kicked open the door. "Don't move or I'll slice your jugul—"

"Maigo?" Terra shrieked from the bed, dropping the book she'd been reading. "What the fuck is wrong with you?"

"Oh, how embarrassing!" Omi trailed away into some corner of my mind.

My pulse didn't come down all at once. It trickled out slowly, like a faucet that couldn't quite turn off. *"I would've stabbed her. I really would've done it. And I wouldn't have stopped until she stopped moving."* I was terrified by who I was becoming, but I had to be social. "Would it be better or worse if I told you I thought you were a trio of violent thieves?"

She sat up, her eyes wide with shock, slowly morphing into fury. "Explain."

"No—fuck that. You explain. Why are you in my house?"

She marched right up to me and squared her shoulders, nose-to-nose. "Do I need permission to lay in your bed now?"

We stood there, glaring. The silent duel of teenagers too proud to blink. Her nose flared. I flared back. Her eyebrows tightened. So did mine. We looked absolutely ridiculous. And we both knew it.

I cracked first. "How much time do you think we have before our parents come back?"

The tension shattered.

Terra dropped to the floor, laughing so hard she gasped for air. "You—" she pointed weakly—"you had.. What is that? Fucking pepper spray?!"

I shrugged with embarrassment. "In case I needed to.. You know.. Blind you or something."

She howled. Rolled on the floor, kicking her legs like a glitching animation.

While she recovered, I set the knives on the desk and pulled out the briefing for the next V9 exercise. The front cover showed an old tribal man, his face painted in white, bone jewelry dangling from stretched earlobes, and a scorched skull hanging from a leather cord around his neck.

The title read: **War of Worlds**.

Terra finally peeled herself off the floor. "What's that?"

"Reading assignment. Next V9 sim."

"You're still doing those?" She sat beside me on the bed, her voice low. "I've been… sick."

She was lying. The hesitation in her voice wasn't illness—it was evasion. But I didn't call her out on it.

"I hope you feel better," I said, resting my hand on her thigh. She didn't flinch.

We sat like that for a moment, pretending her lie wasn't a lie, and that I hadn't come seconds away from stabbing her. Normal teenage things.

"Wait," I finally asked, "what are you doing here?"

"Your mom invited my dad over for dinner." She shrugged. "I tagged along. Don't worry, I didn't come to see you. I just missed Lisa."

I rolled my eyes. "So that's your dad's ride out there?

The one with the file labeled 'Maze Rizen'?"

"Yeah, why?"

My stomach twisted.

"Oh, there's Dad and Lisa!" she pointed.

I followed her gaze out the window. They were pulling into the driveway. My mother—smiling like a TV mom with perfect posture. Mr. Waters beside her. Polished. Charming. Dangerous. The masks of two functioning adults.

"Maigo!" Mom called up the stairs. "Terra! Dinner!"

We looked at each other. An unspoken understanding passed between us.

Next time.

"Maigo, you remember Terra's father, Leigh," Mom said with her smile nailed in place.

"Hi, Mr. Waters." I extended a hand—because that's what polite sons do, even when they're watching you like a hawk for signs of betrayal.

"Look at you!" he said, pulling me in for a rough tousle of my dreads. "I haven't seen you in years. You've gotten so big!"

"Yes," I replied dryly. "Children tend to do that."

"You're such a little taint of a human," Omi scolded. *"Show some manners."*

Terra barely stifled a laugh behind her hand.

Mom disappeared into the kitchen like nothing was wrong, probably to lay out the perfectly curated spread of normalcy she'd been looking forward to all afternoon. That woman could juggle razors in her mouth with a smile on her face.

"Well, I'm gonna help your mother set the table," Leigh said, that same charming glint in his eye. "We'll catch up over dinner."

"Sure thing, Leigh," I echoed back, with just enough venom in my tone to get Omi to flicker nervously.

There was something deeply wrong about him. Something that didn't show up in his soft tone or his easy smile. Something under the skin. His glasses magnified his eyes just enough to distort them, like two fish bowls holding secrets. Maybe it was the folder. Maybe it was the badge. Maybe it was just how smoothly he slid into our lives, like he'd been here all along.

"Sorry," Terra murmured, nudging me once we were alone. "My dad's kind of obsessed with you."

"It's okay," I said, staring past her. "As long as the apple doesn't fall too far."

"*Swing and a miss,*" Omi said smugly.

But it wasn't okay. Not even close.

We sat down for dinner. The table was spotless, candlelit, complete with cloth napkins and a center vase filled with some kind of synthetic lilies. I took my seat across from Mr. Waters and avoided his gaze, but he didn't extend me the same courtesy.

Every time I looked up, he was watching me. Not the casual glancing kind of watching— tracking. Like he was measuring me for something.

I rubbed my eyes, pretended to adjust my telecoms, anything to give myself an excuse not to meet his stare. Eventually, I gave up and focused on my plate.

Mom had brought home a full spread of Japanese takeout. There was tempura, soba, sushi, sashimi, and takikomi rice. It all looked perfect. Too perfect. Like a painting of food rather than real nourishment.

Dessert was the only thing I actually looked forward to: Dragonfire Mochi. A rare flavor from a local place called Kyodain Tokage—The Giant Lizard. Sweet strawberry puree, lemon for contrast, and a burning ginger root core that scorched your tongue like a furnace in velvet. It was a dessert that hurt you on purpose, and I respected that.

The mochi sat in a bowl near Mr. Waters. I was going to have to play his game. "Leigh, could you pass the mochi?" I asked, voice neutral.

"Certainly." He handed me the bowl. "So, Maigo... how's school?"

Shit.

I took a bite to stall. Nodded. Pretended to chew. My mouth was empty in seconds and everyone knew it. Mom raised an eyebrow. Terra tilted her head. Mr. Waters just waited.

"Maigo," Mom said sweetly. "Answer him."

"Okay," I sighed. "School is good."

"What's good about it?" He prodded.

I hated him. I hated how calm he was. I hated that folder in his car and the smile that never cracked. "Well," I said, against every instinct, "I was pulled into the V9 program this week."

Leigh froze. He turned to Mom. "You can't be serious."

She tilted her head, feigning concern. "It'll look good on his college applications, Leigh."

"The V9 program is pre-military," he said sharply. "You know what that means, don't you? It's not school—it's indoctrination. They don't want thinkers. They want operators. They'll desensitize him to violence and turn him into a goddamn drone."

I opened my mouth to argue, but he kept going, this time with less warmth and more weight.

"If your father were here, Maigo... he wouldn't let you set foot in that room."

And there it was. The match. The strike. His words landed like a haymaker to my ribs. I looked down at my plate and saw nothing but static.

My heart jumped into my throat. I wanted to scream about the folder, to force his hand and make him lie to me so I could tear the truth out of his face. But something cold inside me told me that if I pushed, I'd break everything—maybe even Mom. So instead, I looked up at him and said, flatly, "But he isn't here." And I left.

Terra followed me upstairs. "I'm sorry," she whispered.

I couldn't speak. My body was vibrating with rage.

She sat down beside me and ran her fingers along the edge of my jaw. I didn't move. Couldn't.

"Just focus on me," she whispered. Her voice—like mist across the fire. Her hand—like the breeze in a suffocating heat. She was the only thing real enough to hold onto. She laid my head on her lap, pulled a small electric pipe from her pocket, loaded it with something I couldn't read, and turned it on. When she raised it to my lips, I hesitated. "Let me take care of you," she whispered. She took a drag, leaned in, and kissed me. The smoke passed from her lips to mine.

It hit like a bomb going off behind my eyes. Every sense overloaded. My skin pulsed. My chest bloomed with some strange new life, beating harder than it ever had. The kiss was everything: rebellion, sanctuary, salvation. It wasn't a drug—it was a door.

"Terra, we're leaving!" Leigh's voice thundered from downstairs.

She kissed me again, quick and hard. Then she left without a word.

The drug kicked in hard.

My vision folded inward. Sound warped. My eyes stayed open but the world shut off. My arms felt like balloons. My heartbeat became a distant rumor in my ears. I was lifted, flung, reshaped. The room dissolved. The air peeled back. I fell through color and sensation and came to rest in a place I didn't recognize. And that's when the hallucinations began.

My eyes were open, but the world was gone. The walls had peeled away. My bed was no longer a bed, but a tree stump. And the whole world looked like a child's coloring book drawn with shaking hands—skewed perspectives, oversaturated colors, and nothing real beneath the surface.

It felt like I was in someone else's hallucination.

Before me stood a lemonade stand. It was cartoonish, too perfect in its proportions, its lines dancing slightly like a low-res video buffer. Behind it stood a two-dimensional panda cub, bouncing in place. Her tutu was pink and puffy, her head was slightly too large for her body, and her voice sounded like it had been auto-tuned by a sadistic child's toy.

"Hello, Mister!" she chirped. "My name is Prissy the Panda, and I'm selling lemonade so I can buy a brand new tricycle! Will you buy some? It's really good!"

I tried to speak, but my mouth wouldn't move. I couldn't feel my tongue. My jaw. My limbs. My mind was present, but everything else had been turned off. I was locked inside a shell of myself, unable to scream or run or even blink.

"Mister?" Prissy stepped closer. Her blinking eyes were just a little too slow, her head turning a little too far. "Are you okay, Mister?"

My vision blurred at the edges. Color drained from the world.

"Miiister?" Her voice slowed down, pitched lower—glitched. "Do you want to buy some lemonade?"

Everything darkened. The last thing I saw was her innocent panda smile twisting at the corners.

Then the voice came. Male. Calm. Kind of like Leigh's. It filled the black like smoke in a locked room.

"Hello, Maigo."

"Who are you?" I asked, inside myself.

"An old friend."

"What do you want?"

A pause. "I want—"

"What? What do you want?" My voice inside was frantic now, scraping at the walls of this non-reality.

"I want you—"

"Why? Why me?"

"I want you to answer—"

"Answer what?"

"I want you to answer my call."

"What call? What are you talking about?"

"Answer the call, Maigo!"

The voice sharpened, rose into a shriek, and before the sentence could finish—pop—I was back in my room. It was night. I was back. Real.

The soft blue glow of a holo-call lit up my ceiling. Yoen's face was hovering above me, screaming into the ether. "Maigo! Answer me! Stop fucking talking in your sleep!"

The fog cleared from my mind fast. "Sorry," I muttered. "I was taking a nap."

Yoen rolled his eyes. "Doesn't matter. Listen. My dad let me borrow the hover, and one of the seniors told me about an awesome party tonight. So hurry up. We're gonna shut down that fucking AI snitch-bot and get on the circuit."

"Who's he calling snitch-bot?" Omi whined from his corner of my mind.

I rubbed my face, still half-lost in the echoes of Prissy and the voice that wasn't hers. "Alright, thirty minutes."

"I was thinking more like five."

"Why?"

"Because I'm parked outside your house."

Of course he was.

"Okay, five minutes."

I stood up, still unsure what was real, unsure if that voice—that voice—was a figment of my overclocked brain or something far more persistent. All I knew was that the hallucination hadn't come from the drug alone. Something else had gotten in.

Yoen's party was located in a dead part of the industrial ring, inside a pipeline set aside for repair. After a flood damaged the sewage system, the whole sector had been drained and sanitized, supposedly. One of the seniors found out the construction crew wouldn't be back until morning and passed the news down the line.

On the way there, a building caught my eye. It shouldn't have been there.

It was cylindrical, towering, and made entirely of black glass that gleamed with an unnatural smoothness. No address, no entrance, no markings. Just an anonymous shadow among the stubby silhouettes of warehouses and factories. It stood out like a priest at a protest—out of place, but far too confident in its existence.

"You have arrived at your destination," Yoen's hover chirped, far too chipper for where we'd landed.

He parked, but there was no one in sight. No music, no people, not even footprints in the dust. Rows of empty hovers sat abandoned in crooked lines like grave markers. Every building around us was dark. Silent. Watching.

We searched for an entrance—anything that might lead underground. But there was nothing. Just rusted gates and locked access panels.

Yoen tapped his telecom. Tried calling the seniors who had hyped the event. Nothing but static and auto-responders.

With nothing else to do, we slumped onto a nearby bench.

"Well, this was a failure," I muttered. "A big waste of time."

"Maigo," Yoen said, lowering his voice like a prophet about to drop wisdom. "Open SatViz."

"SatViz?" I raised an eyebrow.

SatViz was a hyper-surveillance tool—military grade, civilian accessible for a monthly fee. My mom used it to stream battlefield footage while cooking dinner. Through it, you could see nearly any surface in the world, even look out into space.

"Okay, it's open," I said.

"Search: the dark side of the moon."

"The dark side of the moon," I repeated.

"Unauthorized command," the program responded. "Try again."

I tried again.

Same result.

"It can't be done," Yoen said, smiling. "You can only see the side that reflects light. Might as well not exist." He leaned forward, tapping the metal bench. "So stop wasting your energy focusing on the dark side of everything. Lighten up, man. We're getting into this fucking party."

I grinned. "Alright. What's the plan?"

"Uhh…"

Before he could start, a sleek, pink hover whipped around the corner and drifted hard into the spot across from us. In the passenger seat, a blonde girl with golden skin and ocean-blue eyes smirked through the window. Yoen was immediately love-struck.

But my eyes were on the driver. She was a silhouette at first—tall, dark-haired, steps so light they didn't seem to touch the ground. She moved like she belonged here, like the city had pulled her from its rib and let her walk. Then she stepped under the streetlight and called my name.

"Maigo!" It was Luna.

She ran toward me and hugged me tight. Her arms felt real in a way nothing else had all week.

"Hey," I said. "What are you doing here?"

"I'm here for the Marathon," she said, like it was the most normal thing in the world.

"The what?"

"Come with me." She grabbed my hand and pulled me toward a massive dragon statue on the corner—three heads, six eyes, nine tails.

Its body coiled like a myth unspooling into metal and concrete. She stood before it and opened a holographic program called Members. A one-octave keyboard lit up in the air. Luna played a short, dark melody. The statue's body creaked, gears shifting behind stone.

"Welcome, Rider Luna," a feminine android voice purred.

With a shudder, the dragon's torso cracked open, revealing a stairwell glowing gold.

We descended into the underworld.

At the bottom of the stairs was a giant, hollow pipe, retrofitted like a twisted dream of luxury. Rows of low couches stretched out on either side, each occupied by students in trance. They were half-slumped, half-breathing, wearing strange headsets and plugged into a huge tank labeled Lizard Mist. Gas masks lined the wall like party favors for the damned. The air smelled like mint and oil. Electricity hummed through the floor.

"We're late," Luna said. "Walk faster."

"What the hell is this?" I asked.

Josie, her blonde friend, answered from behind. "You wear the hat, tie the scarf, and check the weather."

"No, that's wrong, Josie," Luna said without missing a beat. "Check the weather, wear the hat, then tie the scarf. Otherwise you'll knock out too early."

"What in the gibberish-fuck are you guys talking about?" Yoen asked.

"You'll see." Josie teased.

We found the last four open seats at the end. I sat beside Luna, Yoen beside Josie.

"Okay," Luna whispered, "step one: check the weather." She paired her telecom to the headgear. "Step two: wear the hat." The headset slid on. "Step three: tie the scarf." She strapped on the mask. The moment it clicked into place, she went limp.

I looked over. Josie and Yoen were already out cold.

The tank hissed. The name "Lizard Mist" stared back at me like a warning disguised as a brand.

I hesitated. Then I reached for the mask. "Check the weather," I whispered to myself, syncing my telecom to the headset. "Wear the hat." I pulled it down over my skull. My fingers hovered over the mask's straps. "...Tie the scarf."

The second the seal clicked, my consciousness was pulled into a drain — spiraling, flipping, dissolving. Colors exploded across my vision like electrical storms inside a kaleidoscope. Then: silence.

When the world reassembled, I was drifting on a pink cloud in a pastel cartoon world that felt like it was drawn by a child high on sugar and existential dread. Everything shimmered. The sky was a spectrum of soft colors with no sun in sight. Dragons — actual dragons — soared overhead, each one saddled by a human rider.

A floating racetrack snaked through the air in the distance, wide and long enough to host a full military parade.

"Maigo!" Luna came into view, gliding toward me on the back of a slim, midnight-blue dragon. Its scales glinted like navy chrome. She looked effortless — like she was born in this space. "Meet Sol," she said proudly, stroking her dragon's neck. "Fastest thing in this sky."

I stared at her like she'd grown wings too. "What is this?"

"This," she said, "is the Lizard Mist Marathon." She reached out a hand. "Hop on."

I didn't hesitate.

Sol's back was warm and smooth beneath me. We took off, slicing through the wind like we had somewhere to be — and we did. Luna was explaining everything as we soared, but the wind scattered her words like confetti. All I caught was:

"New trend… EuroKnights… stolen tech… Sylvain… drugs… music… fun."

That last word landed the hardest.

We banked toward a huge floating platform where others were gathered. I spotted Yoen and Josie already lounging, surrounded by an excited crowd. At their center was someone I didn't expect to see.

Jace Lasaugh.

He waved at Luna. Then looked at me with pure loathing.

"What's his problem?" I asked.

"You killed him."

I squinted, in confusion. "What?"

"In the last sim," Luna clarified. "He was Mentuhotep."

"Oh."

She went on, her tone still casual. "He went off the deep end. Started messing with the staff's powers. At first it was harmless — levitating objects, showing off. Then he lifted Max into the air… dropped him. Caught him. Did it again. Again. Like a toy."

My stomach turned.

"He didn't catch him the last time."

I felt the blood drain from my face.

"Then he threw me in a dungeon. Tortured me. Said I 'needed to see the truth.' I was half-starved and living on rats until you ended the lesson."

I couldn't speak.

"You saved me, Maigo. I haven't thanked you for that yet."

A beat of silence.

"Wanna race?"

"Race?"

She grinned. "Ride with me."

I nodded. Because *what else do you do* after someone tells you they've been psychologically destroyed and want to celebrate with a death-defying sprint through a fantasy sky?

The track stretched 90 kilometers and looked like it had been designed by someone with a vendetta against gravity. Rings of fire. Suspended bear traps. Wild dragon swarms.

An announcer flew above the arena, grinning like a show host on the edge of a breakdown. "Attention racers!" His voice boomed. "Please disregard all safety protocols. Let's fuck shit up!"

The crowd howled. The sky changed. The pastel haze thickened into a deep, reddish fog. The fire turned green. The traps clicked open like jaws waiting to bite.

"I'm not so sure about this," I muttered.

Luna didn't answer. Just gripped Sol's reins tighter.

"5... 4... 3... 2... 1... GO!"

Sol exploded forward.

Wind shredded through us. We twisted through the first fire ring in a blaze of momentum. Sol moved like his life depended on victory — agile, lethal, inspired. Then someone caught up to us. A competitor. Slim build, sharp jaw, cocky sneer.

"That's Sailen Higgs," Luna shouted. "My ex."

Perfect.

He rammed his dragon into ours. The horn cut Luna's leg — deep.

She cried out, gritting her teeth. "Take the reins!"

"What?"

"Take the fucking reins, Maigo!"

I grabbed them. Sol fought me at first, untrusting. We spiraled. The bear traps approached like hungry mouths. I jerked us left, right, barely dodging the snapping steel.

Sailen fired a ball of glowing blue plasma at us. Just as it neared, Luna grunted through the pain, took the reins back, and swerved. We dipped so low we scraped the clouds.

"We're still in this!" she shouted.

The last obstacle loomed ahead: a massive swarm of untamed dragons. Their paths were chaos — darting in every direction like sparks from a fire.

Luna didn't slow down. She climbed higher. Higher. Then looked at me. "Are you ready?"

"No."

"I was talking to Sol."

She stood up on the dragon's back and pulled me to my feet. We were bareback surfing now, wind screaming in our ears.

We dove.

Sol folded his wings over us, cocooning our bodies in slick scale and bone. We cut through the swarm, a bullet wrapped in armor. Dragons snarled as we zipped past, their teeth inches from our faces. Then..

A shadow.

The biggest dragon of them all — black as oil, with metal spikes down its spine — lunged toward us.

Luna screamed. "Now!"

Sol flipped, tossing us skyward as he took the brunt of the hit. We flew through the air, free falling...and landed hard on the finish platform.

Silence. Then a large crowd eruption.

"Ladies and gentlemen, we have a winner of the 4th Lizard Mist Circuit Run! Luna Gray!"

Luna was breathing hard. Her leg was bleeding. But she was smiling. "You can open your eyes now," she teased.

They'd been shut tight since the flip. I opened them. She was inches from my face — eyes sparkling, hair wild from the wind, blood streaked down her calf like war paint. She burst into laughter.

The platform transformed into a dance party. Lights, music, neon fog.

"I'm exhausted," she said, her voice soft now. "Let's get out of here."

I nodded. "How?"

She grinned and stepped back. "Like this." She shoved me.

I fell off the platform into the open sky.

"I'm tired of falling," I thought.

I awoke in the chamber to a loud racket in the distance, coming through one of the pipes.

Luna was still hooked into the cloud. I removed my gas mask, took off the headgear, and headed toward the daunting, metallic orchestra. The closer I got, the more the sounds blended together. When I reached the edge of the chamber, everything was drowned in echo, and reverb. The crashes and bangs harmonized into a sonic haze that sounded like a distant, violent ocean. It was like walking into the edge of a giant seashell. A cool, moist draft gently caressed my skin, and filled the empty space around me. A deep vibration followed, adding a profound low end, and completing the melodic relief I was receiving. But then it hit me.

Fuck.

I sprinted back toward my friends, unplugging as many people as possible along the way. My legs didn't feel like my own. I was sprinting on instinct, lungs raw, every sound drowned by the thunder of water behind me.

"Run! The pipes are flooding!" I warned.

Luna had just woken up, and unplugged the others.

"Maigo, what the fuck I was having fun!" Yoen barked.

"The pipes are flooding. We have to go."

I grabbed Luna and Yoen by the arm, then sprinted toward the exit. Josie followed.

Trailing behind were the strides and screams of our peers who had awakened, from their foggy cloud fantasies, to a lucid nightmare.

A rush of raw sewage busted in, through the pipe. The sealed side of the chamber damned the toxic wave and formed a grimy pool, short-circuiting all of the electrical equipment in the room, including a large plasma battery used to power the circuit's VR engine. Time slowed. Streams of electricity whipped the underground bog in slow controlled strokes, crashing and bouncing away every time they made contact.

The PTSD hit me like a lash to the spine.

Plantation guards held my arms while the whip cracked against my back—again, and again. My breath left me in ragged gasps. The heat. The sting. The feeling of muscle splitting. The sound it made, like air being torn apart.

Electricity slashed across the water like an assassin, swiftly picking off targets, striking bodies mid-escape. It gently kissed metal posts in the sewer, but flash-fried the skin of my classmates. Every scream etched itself into me like tally marks in bone. I couldn't breathe. I couldn't blink.

Excluding my friends, Jace, and a few others, every student that attended that event was electrocuted to death, in a pool of sewer water.

Omi crackled back to life, his voice distorted and too quiet: *"Master Maigo... please have Yoen scramble my memory."* He didn't want to carry it.

Neither did I.

We made it outside—soaked, trembling, and silent beneath the starless glow of the industrial ring's lights.

"Let's get the fuck out of here," I said.

Nobody argued.

When I got home, everything was still.

Mom sat on the couch, face lit by the blue glow of *The Daily News*. The reporters spoke with their usual mixture of urgency and artificial warmth. There were images on the screen—flashes of the industrial ring, wet metal, hazmat suits, a blurred overlay of a pipeline schematic, and beneath it all,

126

a scrolling banner:

"17 students presumed dead in unauthorized VR gathering—incident under investigation."

"Seventeen dead. Eight survivors. One coward."

She didn't hear me come in.

I tried to slip through the kitchen and make it to the stairs, but the volume was lower than usual.

"Maigo?" Her voice was sharp, then softened. "Is that you?"

I froze.

She came around the corner fast, arms already open. Her face—tight, puffy-eyed, covered in drying streaks of mascara—crumbled into relief the moment she saw me. "Oh, honey," she gasped, pulling me into a hug so tight I felt my organs rearrange. "I've been worried sick. I tried calling you a million times, but you didn't answer. I kept thinking the worst. Over and over." She kissed my forehead like I was a child again. It stung in a way I couldn't explain. "Some of the victims went to your school," she said softly, looking at me for any sign of recognition.

I wanted to cry. I wanted to throw up. Instead, I leaned into Omi's advice.

"Don't tell her. She's been through enough tonight."

I kept my tone casual. Detached. "I'm sorry, Mom. I was at Yoen's place, playing his new VR game. Lost track of time." I gave a shrug. "What happened tonight?"

Her face shifted instantly—from worry to protective smile. "Don't worry about it, honey. You should get some rest. We'll talk tomorrow."

I nodded and made my way upstairs. I didn't sleep. I laid there for hours, arms crossed behind my head, replaying every second of the flood. The desperate screams. The blue lightning chewing through waterlogged limbs. The smell. It all bothered me, in an oddly superficial way.

"Am I supposed to feel guilty for this?" I wondered. I didn't feel anything. Not really. But maybe that was the worst part. *"If a pack of lions chases down a herd of gazelles and catches one, the other gazelles don't blame each other because*

they can run fast," I reasoned. *"It's not my fault I survived."* I couldn't believe what I was saying. *"What the fuck is wrong with me?"*

And then—like she could sense the way I was slipping—the only gazelle I'd ever cared about called.

My screen lit up with a familiar face: messy hair, sleepy eyes, warm smile. "Maigo, I was so worried," Terra whispered. Even with her bedhead and restless mug, she was beautiful. "Did you hear what happened?"

"Yeah," I answered. "Speaking of that, I really need to talk to you."

"Whatever you need. I'm just glad you're okay. Talk away."

"No… I think we should talk in person. It's pretty serious."

"Same spot as when we were kids?"

"Yeah. Fourteen-thirty."

"Okay. I'll see you then. Goodnight, Maigo."

"Goodnight, Terra."

She vanished from the screen, and I was left staring at the ghost of her smile.

We used to go to the same cyber-park every summer. Played rocket ball until we were dripping sweat. I'd hover over her on my board and slam the ball every time. Never let her win. She never cared. She liked the fight.

When we got tired, we'd head to the automata trees. Giant steel trunks humming with ozone, purifying the air for the rest of the city. That was the fun part. The way the mechanical branches scooped us up and carried us to the high treehouses where we'd sit for hours, talking about nothing and everything. Just us.

I think that's when I fell in love with her. And I don't think I've ever stopped.

I woke up to the sound of Mom's voice, shrill and urgent. "Maigo! Someone's here to see you!"

I thought it was Terra. I wanted it to be Terra. But when I hit the bottom of the stairs, the weight in the air told me something else.

Leigh Waters was there—red in the face, jaw flexing, eyes darting like loaded guns waiting to fire. He looked like a man rehearsing the act of holding himself together.

Mom stood nearby, arms folded, expression unreadable. Guarded. "Sit down," she ordered, gesturing to the couch.

I did. Leigh sat beside me, still breathing hard through his nose. He planted his face in his hands, elbows on knees, and just... sat there. Time became a vacuum. No sound. No motion. Just the weight of what wasn't being said.

Then, quietly—dead calm—he spoke. "Maigo. I am trying very hard to contain myself. Please, be honest with me." A beat. "Did you have sex with Terra?"

Fuck.

The air left my lungs like I'd been gut-punched. I couldn't speak. I couldn't lie. I just nodded.

Leigh stood up and began pacing, hands on his hips, his tall frame moving like a lion caged for the first time. Controlled fury. He kept stopping and starting, running his fingers through his hair.

I hadn't realized how big he was until now. Not just physically—his presence filled the room like a pressure change.

"Okay," he muttered. "Okay. Thank you for being honest." He looked at me with something between sorrow and contempt. "That means something."

I started to speak. "Mr. Waters, I'm sorr —"

"Don't speak, Maigo," Mom cut in sharply.

Leigh lowered himself back onto the couch, but didn't look at me. "Maigo, I understand that these things happen. I was sixteen once too. That's me giving you empathy." He took a long, slow breath. His eyes glistened. "Now I need you to hear me—and return the favor." He looked over at Mom for a second. Her eyes were fixed on the floor. "I know you and Terra have gotten close. We're almost like family..." he trailed off, voice cracking slightly. "But I have to do what's best for her." The pause before the next words was surgical. "From now on, you will have no contact with her." His words hit me like a switchblade. "I won't be bringing her with me to visit anymore. Her telecoms have your ID number blocked. And I came here today to make sure you harbor no confusion about why I made this decision." He looked me dead in the eyes. "Do you understand?"

My throat clenched. I could barely get the words out. "I understand, Mr. Waters."

He nodded, like it hurt him more than it hurt me. "Thank you. You're a good kid, Maigo. I'm sorry I had to be the one to teach you this difficult life lesson." He got up and left.

Mom started in immediately. She had her own version of the "what were you thinking" speech prepared, full of disappointment and parental expectations. But I didn't hear a single word of it.

The moment Leigh walked out, everything else went quiet. All I could think about was Terra. Her laugh. Her eyes. The way she looked at me like I was something in a world that mostly made me feel like nothing. And now she was gone.

My chest tightened like someone had stuffed it full of broken glass and hit it with a hammer. I couldn't breathe. My limbs went numb. It was a sensation like dying—but slower.

When Mom finally stopped yelling, I didn't say anything. I just walked to my room, laid on my bed, and shut the world out.

I didn't get up again until the next day.

I was halfway down the stairs when Mom called out, "Maigo! Someone's here to see you."

I moved faster, hoping — stupidly — to see Terra.

Instead, I found Doctors Light and Cobb sitting perfectly still in our living room, like mannequins pressed from polished plastic and carbon fiber. My stomach dropped.

"Good morning, Mr. Rizen," Cobb said, rising to his feet with the stiffness of someone who forgot how to be human. "We need you to get dressed and come with us."

"Why?"

"Don't panic," Light added quickly. "You'll only be gone a couple hours. We just have a few questions."

I folded my arms. "You two only get to ruin my life Monday through Friday. It's the weekend. I have plans."

Mom spoke without turning her head. "Just go with them, honey. It'll be fine." Her tone didn't match her words. Her eyes were tired. That worry, that fragile mask of order — it was barely hanging on.

I went upstairs and got dressed, then followed them out to a matte-black hover waiting in the street. The ride was silent. Cobb stared at the sky. Light occasionally glanced at me. My eyes wandered.

They took me deep into the military ring, to a building that looked like it had been designed with zero regard for human emotion. Steel walls. No windows. AI Guardians out front with arm-cannons and shoulder-mounted plasma blades that hummed as I walked by. I felt the heat from them in my bones.

Inside, they led me through an endless maze of sterile hallways before stopping at a door labeled: **O-6 Haines.**

Cobb looked at me. "Enter. She's waiting."

I opened the door and stepped inside.

A tall woman in a charcoal-grey pantsuit stood beside a desk. Her hair was pulled so tightly into a bun it looked like it hurt. She didn't smile. "Good morning, Mr. Rizen," she said. "I'm Colonel Sarah Haines, commanding officer of the Los Mitos Peacekeeping Unit." She gestured for me to sit with all five fingers — the kind of wave you do when you're used to people obeying the first time.

I sat.

She opened a folder, flicked through a few holographic documents, and sighed like this whole thing was a waste of her time. "According to our GPS data, you were in the industrial district at the time of the sewer incident. Would you like to explain that?"

I swallowed hard. *The tracker. Fuck. I forgot about the tracker.*

"I didn't do anything bad," I said, voice higher than I wanted it to be. "I promise, I— I didn't even know it was that kind of party."

Haines didn't blink. "You entered restricted municipal infrastructure. You used unauthorized virtual narcotics supplied through black-market channels. You helped shut down a government-monitored AI unit. You participated in an unsanctioned VR event that led to the deaths of seventeen minors. And your only response is 'I didn't do anything bad?'"

My mouth dried out instantly. "I didn't know. I didn't know it was going to happen like that."

She leaned forward, eyes cold and clinical. "You didn't want to know. That's the difference." She let the silence in the room thicken the air. "Answer my questions plainly. What kind of party was it?" she asked flatly. "Were there drugs?"

I hesitated. Then nodded. "It was like a race or something. There were these—headsets, and gas masks. They were connected to this big tank labeled 'Lizard Mist.' I didn't know what it was."

"You didn't ask?"

"No one knew. Or they pretended not to."

She locked eyes with me and didn't let go. "That substance was developed by a paramilitary organization currently under investigation for distributing mind-altering tech in high schools. You got high on stolen tech designed by enemies of the state, and then abandoned your classmates in a death trap."

Her words echoed like gunshots inside my skull.

"I tried to save them," I said. "I unplugged people. I ran. I tried—"

"You survived. That's all the file says. It doesn't say 'tried.' It says you ran."

That sentence stuck in my chest like a nail. I felt Omi stir inside my neural interface but he didn't say a word.

"Am I going to jail?" I asked.

Colonel Haines stared at me for a moment longer, then leaned back in her chair and smiled for the first time. It wasn't comforting. It didn't reach her eyes. It wrapped around her face like a barbed wire necklace, barely containing something feral. "No," she said. "We don't waste young talent like you on incarceration." She pulled up a new file, and rotated the display so I could see it. The screen showed the V9 program roster, with my face highlighted in blue. "You're already green-lit," she said. "Doctor Cobb marked you as a top candidate for our Summer Leadership Initiative. We call it the SLI, but the name doesn't matter." She tapped once and a list of names appeared, some familiar, some not. "These are the other students we're evaluating for special placement. You'd train with Peacekeeping units, gain access to tactical infrastructure, high-level archives, even field simulations. You'd be part of something great."

I leaned back in my chair, bile creeping up my throat. "And if I say no?"

Her voice softened, but somehow became more terrifying. "Then we file a full report. Your GPS logs. Your communication logs. Your SatViz history. Your presence at the Lizard Mist site with unquestionable evidence. We can make that story sound however we want it to. And maybe you'd do okay in juvenile detention for a while, but when that file gets passed around to the colleges and employers and ID evaluators... well, let's just say it gets harder to be a model citizen." She stood up and walked to the door, opening it. "But if you say yes," she continued, "then you and your friends' records will be cleaned. You keep your spot in the V9 program. And you get a future that looks a lot more like opportunity... and a lot less like punishment."

I stood, fists clenched at my sides. "You're blackmailing me," I said.

She smiled again. "No, Maigo. I'm giving you a way out. A choice."

I stared at her. *"There is no 'choice.' There never was. Just which knife you want stuck in your side."* Then, without speaking, I signed the document she sent to my telecoms ID. My name glowed across the bottom of the consent form.

"Good," she said. "Someone from my team will be in touch soon. You're free to go."

As I walked down the hall, Doctor Cobb and Light waited at the exit. They didn't say anything at first. We rode back to my house in near-silence.

But halfway through the drive, I asked the question that had been churning in my gut for weeks. "How do people decide what's right or wrong?"

Light kept his eyes on the road. Cobb didn't answer right away.

"Good and bad seem to vary from person to person," he said. "Some think there's an objective moral truth — that hurting someone innocent is always wrong, or taking what doesn't belong to you is always wrong." Then he turned to me, eyes suddenly human in a way I hadn't seen before. "I think deciding what's right or wrong… is just another way we pretend our selfishness is righteous."

Dr. Light swerved sharply.

"Indus, look at the fucking road." Cobb squealed.

I laughed. "Well, damn. Even Cobb drops f-bombs."

We laughed the rest of the ride home, but the weight of it all followed me like a shadow. I was sixteen years old. I'd just watched people die. I'd been blackmailed by the military. I was being groomed into a system I barely understood.

And the worst part? A part of me felt important for the first time in my life. There was no difference between survival and purpose.

Chapter 4

SURVIVAL INSTINCTS

"*W*atch out, Master Maigo!*" Omi's warning barely had time to register before a blur of motion sliced through the morning haze.

A man on hover skates ripped down the sidewalk, weaving between pedestrians like a phantom, flames licking from the burners at his heels. His dreadlocks whipped behind him, his arms pumping with manic energy.

A trio of Peace Officers gave chase, their armored legs pounding hard against the pavement. One of them launched a grappling claw, but the man bent backward mid-glide, letting it sail harmlessly over him. He twisted, grabbed the tether, yanked hard, and sent the P.O. sprawling. Another dove at him, but he popped an aerial 360, slammed a plasma-powered kick into the officer's chest-plate, and sent him crashing into a newsstand.

The third officer hesitated. That moment of doubt gave the fugitive all the space he needed.

As he zipped past me a second time, he gave a nod and a grin that felt mythic. "I still got it," he said, then vanished down the street.

I stood frozen. All I could do was whisper, "Wow."

The Peace Officers regrouped, humiliated and seething. One of them shoved me aside. "Move along, kid!"

And just like that, it was over. Another glitch in the smooth surface of the city, gone before it could be analyzed.

When I walked into the V9 classroom, I stopped short.

Terra was already at our table.

She looked—perfect. Not her usual effortless-perfect, but staged-perfect. Coiled hair bouncing in programmed waves. Skin glowing like high-end ceramic. Subtle makeup sculpting her cheekbones just enough to hurt. And her scent—sweet, electric, intentional.

She glanced at me, then looked away. A brief silence catalyzed her anxious energy, forcing her to spill. "Before you say anything, I'm sorry about my dad," she said quietly. "He found my comms log. I got grounded. Still can't see you outside of school, but I talked him into letting me enroll in V9."

My heart was racing, but my mouth forgot how to speak.

She tilted her head. "I don't even care about this stupid program. I just didn't want to lose you."

Before I could find words, a hand brushed my cheek.

"Good morning, handsome," Luna purred as she passed, voice dipped in velvet.

My pulse went nuclear.

"Oh boy!" Omi chirped. *"I love triangles!"*

I didn't dare look at Terra, but I could feel the rage radiating from her direction.

Then the doctors entered, Cobb with his usual puppet-show enthusiasm. "Ms. Waters!" He beamed. "Welcome aboard. This morning's lesson is a survival scenario. I trust you remember the protocol?"

"Perfectly," Terra said, masking the storm inside.

"Excellent! Students, assume your positions. I'd like to begin immediately."

No time for explanations. No time to fix the mess. The chest closed over me. Darkness swallowed the classroom, and the jungle began.

The lesson was set in sixteenth century Amazonia. The juniors were all placed as part of a large native tribe that recently made contact with a Portuguese exploration unit. Dr. Cobb told us that our objective was to "survive by any means necessary." Such ominous direction put us all on edge before we even loaded in. My point of entry was a meeting between high-ranking members of the Parakanã nation.

"Children of the Amazon, I have summoned you to make a very important choice." The chief spoke in a perfectly tuned baritone. "The shores, just outside of our beloved rainforest, have been lodged by an armed troop of fair-skinned men. Some members of our tribe have made contact with their scouting party. They say that they are trapped between land and sea, sick, and running out of resources. The one they call Capelo has asked us to help them navigate through the forest to find food and medicine. I must refer to those I trust most, to make such a decision."

An elderly woman with blood-derived face paint stood up immediately to speak. "Chief Guarani, if the forest wanted guests, she would invite them in herself - yes. Instead, she has cursed them all with shoreline purgatory. We cannot ignore such simple truths - no." She paused from ad-libbing herself to drink from her cup, then wiped a thick mucosal substance from her mouth. "We have survived this long by keeping a close ear to her whispers - yes. Let their fate be woven."

She was challenged by a large muscular man.

"I respectfully disagree, Kaoworara-Mayana." He demonstrated such a calm seriousness in his speech. "I think we should attack them while they are weak. These men are from a foreign world and cannot be trusted. Their intentions are as sure as Ocelot cries, and we are not gullible simians. I understand that they are in need of help, but who knows what they will do once they've regained their strength. The safety of our people must come first, so they cannot continue such close habitation. If we kill them all now, they won't have anyone to send home for help."

A scout soldier stood up slowly with his head hanging from his shoulders. His vulnerable disposition froze time for everyone in the room. "Wari-Borkana, I don't think you understand what we're up against. Our soldiers are mere game to them. Our weapons are playthings. These men are tall, stout and carry sticks that shoot lightning. I hear whispers that more of them have landed further north and their spirits carry great sickness within them. Many of our neighbors to the north are dying after negligible interaction with them. I have seen with my own eyes, a foe we cannot defeat. Mayana is right. Leave them alone."

"You have always been a coward, Abaya," Borkana hissed.

"And you have always been a fool, Borkana," Mayana quickly retorted.

"May I remind you both that the lives of 1000 Parakanã rest in your hands." The Chief interrupted with a disappointed disposition. "If your mouths have nothing of value to offer, I must ask that you lend your ears instead. Disrespect this council again, and I will take them myself."

The room got really tense, and no one else spoke up so I decided to put my two cents in. "We could trick them." The whole group stared at me with intrigue. I turned to Borkana. "They are too powerful to fight, even in their current state. So we can't just run to the beach and try to raze the settlement." I swapped my gaze to Mayana. "If we don't help them at all, more might come and attack us for letting their friends suffer. Right now, they are desperate and we know just how cruel the jungle can be. Let's pretend to help them, set up a trap and lead them to it."

Everyone in the room seemed receptive to my idea. The members suggested various ways to entice them, and locations that were especially fatal for outsiders. Borkana apologized to Abaya and Mayana with a musk-ridden hug. All of the anger and rigidity in the room seemed to melt into dedicated cooperation.

While they worked out all of the details, I returned my focus to the brand new disaster unfolding in my real life. *"How am I going to make things right with Terra?"* I pondered. *"I can't tell her about that night. It would kill her. But if I lie and she finds out from someone else, it'll be way worse."*

I debated back and forth with myself for a while before finally deciding to tell her the truth. I just knew I couldn't do it in the V9 classroom with the forces of public embarrassment working against us. It wouldn't be fair to Terra and it certainly wouldn't help my case. I had to figure out another way.

"So it is settled," Chief Guarani interrupted. "You will lead a team of our best to trick the invaders into the depraved streams to the west. They may be strong but their blood cannot resist the venom of Lara's aquatic arachnids. You must convince them to travel as one across the streams and make sure they do not get out of the water until every single one has been bitten."

"Understood." I accepted. "When will my team be ready?"

"You will all be christened for this task at tonight's ritual." Guarani answered.

When the night came, hundreds of villagers gathered around a giant fire well, dug deep into the ground and blazing high above our heads. There was a wooden cross-section arched around the flame, bound by a living hemp vine. My eyes tracked the extra fibers attached to a crank and lever machine designed to lower and raise heavy objects and I quickly got jacked on anxiety.

As the ceremony went on, I continued to catastrophize - gathering anecdotal evidence for my fears. *"Are they going to dip me into that fire pit?"* I gripped my chest.

There were fast drums perfectly predicting the cadence of my cowardice heartbeat. *"How are they doing that?"* My nails dug deep into my chest.

Bamboo instruments blew deep waves of sinister melodies that overwhelmed my amygdalic alarm system. *"I'm gonna die."*

The fire roared - refocusing my attention. *"Is that blood in her cup?"* I got lost again.

Mammalian cries sang from the forest over the disturbed orchestra. *"Ocelot or Capuchin?"* My mind felt like it was being kicked around a soccer field. This went on for at least five minutes.

"Children, feast!" Chief Guarani decreed as ten skewered tapir carcasses rose from the giant oven.

Every ounce of strength drained from my body in a relieving sigh. *"Of course, it's for food."* I laughed out loud to myself.

After everyone got their portion, the music stopped and the chief called our team up to him. I could immediately tell that the other three members were my classmates because they just looked like themselves as tribesmen. It was purely comical to see Yoen's ugly bowl cut on a shredded tribal body.

Guarani gave a long speech about the history of their tribe's survival and our plan to trick the Portuguese. It was a beautifully orated narrative, but one particular piece reignited my fright.

"When the pale men are dead, you must spend the remainder of the night in the unwalked forest. We must make certain that you have not received their illness. If you return without taking the proper precautions, we will be forced to kill you on sight." Chief Guarani looked directly at me while delivering this dire news. "Before Kuat rises, you will make your way toward the shore to meet the lightning throwers. Our scouts have already made arrangements with them to follow you." He didn't even ask if we had questions before reviving the party.

The Parakanã danced deep into the night, but we checked out early to rest for the long day ahead.

Morning came too fast.

We met the Portuguese exploration party at the edge of the jungle. There were way more of them than I anticipated, and less than half of them looked like soldiers. Capelo greeted us with pure joy and excitement, then signaled for everyone else to follow us.

We started our journey on a burn trail that ran near the village. We could feel the forest's eyes watching from a distance. I noticed a woman and two children at the end of the line.

She was tall, and carried a large brush knife. Despite her brutish appearance, the way she softly guided her children revealed her tender nature. A small man with a large growler accompanied her. They didn't interact much on the trail. He drank and occasionally yelled at her. She watched the kids, and tried her best to diffuse him.

About halfway through our journey, his aggression became more frequent and her soothing techniques stopped working. Their system broke down and became a tactile argument. Her need to defend herself overshadowed her observation duties and her son chased his sister away from the burn trail.

"Oh, no." I rushed toward them in a panic, prompting Terra to follow.

The jungle floor was dense and it felt impossible to track them.

In the distance, I could hear the little girl's sonar cries and followed them to their location. She had fallen and scraped her knee on the ground. Her brother stood over her, unsure what to do.

Our frenzied energy must've alerted other party members to follow us - including the parents. Their mother had this mixed look of relief and fatigue. We responded to her with disappointed miens and carried her children right past her. She didn't protest.

Terra and I took the boy and girl to the front of the group and cared for them like they were our own.

They didn't speak a word of our language, but they responded to the comfort we provided. I kept picking them up and flying them above my head like little macaws. Terra was picking fruits along the way and keeping them happy with succulent sweet treats.

It was almost like a glimpse into the future of the family we could have. I felt such wholesome warmth every time I watched Terra interact with those kids. She would smile so wide and get glossy eyes when she did. To this day, I wish that trail was a little bit longer, just so I could keep seeing her that way.

When we arrived at the stream, Yoen stopped the crowd and made harsh eye contact with me. He started directing the explorers to get in the stream and pointing at a nearby burn trail that it led to. They blindly obeyed and entered the elbow-high water. It was hard to watch. I stood on the bank, toward the front of the group, and watched the deadly opaque arachnids bite the early adopters. After the first person collapsed, they all started to scream. By this time, there was no amount of panic or protest that could save them. All but four of the Portuguese explorers had been bitten.

The air was thick enough to drink, humid and sour with ferocious plant pheromones. My small bit of clothing stuck to my skin, plastered with sweat. Each footstep squelched against the mud, the forest floor pulsing like a living lung beneath us. The stream ahead gurgled with a slow treacherous promise. The jungle thanked us for its meal.

The two children were still with Terra and me, so they hadn't entered the stream yet. Their parents unintentionally stalled their fates by lagging behind the group in an intense argument. By the time they caught up, the father had realized what was happening and was loading his rifle.

Yoen noticed his hostility and rushed toward him to disarm him. Jade assisted, by holding him while Yoen struck him repeatedly. He was tough and much larger than them. After absorbing a few full power blows to the face, he managed to shake one of his arms free and counter Yoen's assault with his own. He struck Yoen with the butt of the rifle, knocking him to the ground. He quickly shifted his focus to Jade. The man threw her to the ground and aimed his rifle at her. Before he could get a shot off, Yoen sprung up and punctured his neck with a small utility blade then drug it 180 degrees through his flesh - successfully subduing the threat.

In the calm of their scuffle's aftermath, the mother dropped to her knees pleading for mercy. "Por favor!" She cried. "Meus filhos!"

"Shut up you fucking beggar!" Yoen silenced the woman.

Too familiar.

Yoen grabbed her son from Terra and presented him as leverage. He pointed to the stream to signify that he wouldn't return her child unless she entered.

She complied.

Yoen handed the boy over as promised then turned his gaze to me. The little girl took shelter behind me.

"Maigo, I know how you get in these simulations. I get it. It looks real. But it's not." Yoen empathized. "Give me the girl, or we will lose."

I looked at the girl clenching my leg like a capuchin infant to its mother. She latched onto my leg with surprising strength, fingers digging into my calf like tiny claws.

Her body trembled against mine, a shivering animal instinctively clinging to the bigger creature.

I could feel the heat of her skin — fear pouring off her like steam — even through the simulated layers of our different worlds.

I looked back at Yoen. Then I looked at the mother, who's eyes wished at least one of her children would survive. I looked back at Yoen, again. "I can't." I protested.

Without hesitation, Yoen sprinted toward me with hostility. I tossed the girl to Terra and braced for a fight. Yoen took me down immediately and started dropping strikes. I caught one and flipped him over to take the top position. Just as I cocked my arm back to hit him, I heard a splash. We both looked up in disbelief. Terra had tossed the girl into the stream.

The splash sounded too small for what it was. A child's life, disappearing in a ripple. I didn't breath. I didn't blink. I just stared at the water, wishing I could reverse the moment with a thought. *With a prayer?*

I couldn't look away as the little girl flailed her arms in the water, struggling to stay afloat. I heard her little screams which were quickly cut off by choking and muffled by her descent below the surface.

The silence in the aftermath was chilling.

Nobody moved or spoke for several minutes after she stopped struggling.

I couldn't stop picturing her ghost staring at me. Begging me to save her.

The silence was interrupted by Jade's shriek! "Ow! I think I got bitten." Jade was holding her foot.

"Let me see it," Terra was quick to her aide.

The bite had already turned black. The wound festered in front of our eyes. The skin around it had turned the color of overripe plums, and blood leaking out smelled rancid.

"I know what to do. We have to take her to the oasis spring. It can heal the wound. We have to move fast," Terra called out. "The venom's spreading."

Jade's foot was blackening quickly. The bite had broken open and was leaking dark blood down her ankle. She was shivering violently. Whatever was inside her was moving fast.

Yoen hacked a path forward with a machete he'd picked up from the invaders. "I don't think she's got long."

"She just needs to hold on until we reach the spring." Terra's determination countered my skepticism.

"You sure this spring even exists?"

"Yes," Terra answered sharply. "The elders told me about it yesterday. They say life first crawled out of those waters. The right temperature, the right minerals. Something about the pH preserves the regenerative compounds. Like a cradle for meristem cells."

Yoen glanced back. "Stem cells?"

"Basically. Think of it like a wild soup of organ-building precursors. Like the ones in the labs back home—except untouched. Raw."

"That's… kind of incredible," I admitted.

"We can't waste time. If we don't drain the venom, it'll hit her major organs," Terra said, voice flat with urgency. "And even if we do, the tissue damage—"

"Don't finish that thought." Yoen couldn't even consider the thought of Jade dying. Or maybe it was the prospect of losing.

The jungle shifted around us. Insects buzzed violently in the trees. Birds shrieked and fled to the canopy.

"Something's coming," Yoen warned. He stopped. Held out a hand. We froze.

Something slithered across the path, thick as a tree trunk. Its body was patterned in a shadowy mosaic of green and black. It stopped. Raised its head above the grass.

"Anaconda," I whispered.

It uncoiled, slowly, like a monstrous spring stretched to its ends. Its eyes shimmered gold. We backed up, Jade limp in Yoen's arms now. She wasn't conscious anymore.

The snake lunged. Leaves exploded around us, a green firestorm of torn vines and shredded bark. The ground shook with every undulation of the creature's body. A muscle as long as a bus and twice as unforgiving.

"Run!"

We scattered. I bolted near Terra through a dense patch of ferns. Behind us, I heard a crashing sound—Yoen slashing at the creature's flank. It hissed.

It stopped chasing but we didn't stop running. We couldn't.

The jungle narrowed, then opened wide. Steam curled from the earth, hanging in the humid air like silk. We had reached it. The oasis.

It was an otherworldly pool—milky blue, shallow and still. The stones surrounding it were smooth and bone-white. Moss clung to the walls. Steam curled off the surface in lazy tendrils, carrying the tang of wet stone and old, secret minerals.

We placed Jade on the edge. Terra knelt beside her, pulled out the last of her vines and herbal wraps.

"We need to drain the venom."

"Like, cut it out?" Yoen asked.

"No. Pressure and heat will help draw it. The rest…" She reached into the water, scooped some, and tasted it. "It's alive."

Gross.

We dipped her foot into the pool.

Jade didn't wake, but her body flinched. Her leg twitched. The blackness had spread to her calf. We waited in silence.

The jungle pressed in close, but none of us spoke. We didn't need to.

Say you're sorry. Say you panicked. Say something that makes me believe you're still you.

But she didn't.

I turned to Terra, knives sharpened. "You didn't have to throw her."

Terra didn't look at me. She watched the water move against Jade's skin. "She could've been one of the seniors," she said quietly. "Maybe Luna."

I blinked. "What?"

She looked up now. Something hard in her eyes. "I know what happened that night. You think Yoen can keep a secret? Please."

The air between us became heavier than the jungle. I opened my mouth. Closed it. Tried again. "You think that makes what you did okay?"

"She was a simulation, Maigo."

"She was a child."

Terra stood. "Don't pretend you know the difference anymore. You've changed, Maigo."

We didn't speak again.

We stayed by the spring until morning. Jade's breathing stabilized. Her leg still looked bad, but the spreading had stopped. The pool had done something. Maybe even enough.

By the time the sun cut through the canopy, the forest felt lighter. The danger had passed.

When we returned to the village, the celebration was already underway. Our deception had worked. The Parakanã were safe. The mission, as far as the program was concerned, was a success.

But Terra was gone.

By the time I crawled out of the V9 chamber, there was no sign of her.

Cobb paced by the wall, smiling proudly. "Well done. You survived."

"Barely," I muttered.

Yoen leaned against his pod, chewing gum with that unbothered grin. "I can't wait for the next round." Yoen had top marks and got to choose the next lesson. "Next stop: the Chinese Boxing Revolution."

School had ended. The halls were flooding with students. I moved slower than the rest, dragging my feet down the hall, distracted by the static in my chest. What happened in that simulation — what Terra did — it wasn't fading like the others. The screams still clung to the folds of my brain. So did the silence that followed.

"Hey, desert prince."

I looked up.

Luna stood leaning against the wall beside the exit, arms crossed, hip cocked to the side, chewing on a piece of bright red gum like she was half-aware of its flavor. "You look like you just crawled out of a mass grave. Want to talk about it?"

I shrugged. "Only if the grave's in a rainforest and the headstones are innocent children."

"That bad, huh?" She started walking. I followed. "Come over after school. Josie's mom is off-planet and the place is quiet. You can decompress… or vent, or do that thing where you pretend nothing's wrong until your mouth betrays you."

good." I glanced at her. "You're disturbingly

"I'm disturbingly good at a lot of things," she smirked. "But mostly reading boys who might be attached to the wrong girl."

I stopped walking. "You think I'm into the wrong girl?"

She stopped too, turning to face me. "I think you're with a girl who made a choice that broke something in you. And now you don't know whether to blame her or yourself for still caring."

I didn't say anything. We started walking again.

"Look, I'm not trying to steal you or anything," she lied, expertly. "Just… offering you a place where you don't have to perform."

"Perform?"

168

"You know. Be the stoic little soldier for Terra. Be the guy who forgives the unforgivable because he doesn't want to lose her."

I followed her out of the building. "She killed a little girl, Luna."

"I know."

"Like, tossed her into the stream. Just— gone. She didn't even hesitate. And I can't stop asking myself if I would've done the same, if the kid was in my arms. And the worst part—"

"You're still in love with her," Luna finished.

I nodded.

She didn't say anything for a while. We reached the curb. The hover she'd been borrowing was parked half-in-shadow, humming softly.

"I'm not asking you to stop loving her," she said, finally. "I'm just saying, maybe give yourself a place to breathe."

I glanced at her. The way the sunlight caught the edge of her lashes, the barely-there curve of a smirk, the way she didn't rush me to answer. Terra was fire and adrenaline. Luna was gravity. Dangerous in a quieter way.

"I'll come over," I said. "But just to decompress."

She opened the passenger door for me. "Sure," she said with a sly smile. "Just to decompress."

Josie's apartment was on the fifth floor of a tower block in the outer ring — not fancy, but not crumbling either. The hallway smelled like incense and cleaning fluid. Luna punched in the code, the door slid open, and warm, golden light spilled across the welcome mat.

Inside, it was quieter than I expected. Muted synth playing from hidden speakers. Curtains drawn. A few glowing planters glowing softly near the kitchenette. She walked in like she lived there.

"Shoes off," she said, kicking hers under the couch. "We leave the world at the door."

I followed, dropping onto a sunken couch that swallowed me in cushions. She tossed her jacket onto a hook, then moved to the kitchen, grabbing two glasses and something that looked halfway between tea and bioluminescent syrup.

"So what now?" I asked. "Do I just start crying or do you have an emotional questionnaire I'm supposed to fill out?"

Luna snorted, bringing me a glass. "No crying. Unless it helps." She settled next to me, tucking one leg beneath herself. "But if you want to talk, talk."

I stared into the liquid, watching the pale purple light swirl when I tilted the glass. "She didn't even blink," I muttered. "That's what keeps getting me. Like... Terra didn't hesitate. She didn't wrestle with it. She just did it."

Luna didn't respond right away. She just took a sip of her drink and waited.

"I knew what we were doing was ugly," I continued. "We all did. But I thought... I don't know. That there'd be a line."

"Some people are good at ignoring lines," Luna said softly.

I looked at her. "She said the girl could've been a senior. Said it might've been you."

There it was. A flicker behind her eyes. A flash of hurt. "Wow," she said, leaning back. "That explains a lot."

I waited for her to say more, but she didn't. Her face was neutral, but her jaw had gone tight.

"She knows," I said. "About you and me. The night after the... the sewer."

"She doesn't know know. She's guessing. Jade overheard a joke and probably ran her mouth. Terra's smart. She can connect dots."

"You mad?"

Luna looked at me, really looked, with that unnerving clarity she had when she dropped the games. "No," she said. "I just wish it didn't have to be a secret. Or a mistake."

I felt heat rise in my chest. "I didn't say it was a mistake."

"You didn't have to."

Silence pulsed between us, and something electric twisted in it — shame, want, guilt, pull. I watched her fingers circle her glass. She never looked away.

"She makes me feel alive," I said. "Like I'm on fire."

Luna nodded. "And I make you feel what? Safe?"

"You make me feel... like I'm allowed to be a fucking person again."

That hit her. I saw it. She moved closer. Our knees touched. Her voice dropped to a whisper.

"You don't have to pick, you know. Not yet."

I swallowed. "But I will, eventually."

"Eventually," she echoed. "But not tonight."

I don't know who leaned in first. Maybe both of us. Her breath tasted like citrus and nerve. Her lips hovered just above mine, waiting. Inviting, not begging.

I didn't kiss her. But I didn't move away either.

We stayed like that for a while — suspended.

"I should go," I said.

She nodded. "I know."

I couldn't tell you how much time passed before I left.

The streets were quieter than usual. Too quiet. No buzz of late-night hovers, no teenagers laughing in alleyways. Just the hum of street lamps and the whisper of neon reflecting off wet pavement. My footsteps echoed like accusations in the stillness.

I shoved my hands in my pockets and stared straight ahead, trying not to think about the warmth of Luna's apartment. Or how close I'd come to staying. Or how her breath had tickled my lips like she belonged there.

"You know," Omi said softly, his voice cutting into the quiet. *"Your heart is not a battlefield. You don't have to burn everything down just to figure out what you want."*

"I didn't ask."

"No, but you're spiraling."

I kicked a loose pebble and watched it skitter across the pavement. *"She killed a little girl."*

"Yes. And you're still trying to forgive her for it."

I stopped walking. *"I can't forgive her. But I also can't stop… remembering who she was before. The way she looked when she fed those kids. The way she laughed on the trail. That person is still in there. Right?"*

"Maybe," Omi said. *"But maybe that person was never real to begin with. Sometimes love is projection, Maigo. You hold up a mirror, and hope the person you see is the one looking back."*

I stared at the ground, letting the words sink in. "I don't want to be alone," I said out loud.

"You're not."

I scoffed. *"Easy for an AI to say."*

"I may be code, but I know you better than anyone else. I've watched you grow up. I've seen every tantrum, every triumph. And right now, what you need isn't love or clarity — it's grace. For yourself."

I let out a shaky breath. The cold air bit at my skin, but Omi's voice had a warmth that somehow dulled the edge.

"Thanks," I said, barely audible.

"Anytime, son."

And that word — *son* — hit harder than anything else. I was torn between accepting the warmth of Omi's affection and recognizing that he was programmed to do so. Lately, it had seemed like more than just a job to him. It started feeling like he genuinely cared for me. Even if it wasn't real, he made me feel protected. And that was enough.

I didn't respond. Just kept walking until home was in sight, the city lights dimming behind me.

When I stepped through the door, the lights were already dimmed. The house felt... wrong. Like it had exhaled and forgotten how to breathe again.

I kicked off my shoes and rounded the corner to the living room.

Mom was there. Not *Lisa* — not the polished politician, not the radiant leader of clean ambition and victory speeches. Just Mom. Her hair was wild, tangled like seaweed in a storm. Her makeup had been rubbed away in streaks, revealing cracked skin beneath tear-scorched cheeks. Her robe hung loosely, cinched carelessly at the waist. Around her were scattered piles of ancient family photos, some still inside brittle albums, others loose and bent at the corners.

She was staring at a picture — one of the three of us. Dad had me hoisted on his shoulders, and Mom was laughing at something just outside the frame. It was the kind of smile that didn't come back.

"Mom?" I said softly.

Her head didn't move, but her fingers tightened around the photo. She inhaled, sharp and sudden. "I was beautiful once," she whispered. "I used to have… everything."

I stepped toward her, unsure of how to move in a space that suddenly felt sacred and fragile. "You still do," I offered, sitting beside her. "You still have me."

She turned, just enough for me to see the depth in her eyes — a raw pit of guilt, grief, and unbearable shame. "You weren't supposed to see me like this," she said. "I didn't want… this version of me to survive anymore."

I placed my hand on hers, gentle. "We're surviving together."

She pulled away. Not cruelly — more like a child retreating from scalding water. "Go to your room, Maigo."

"Mom—"

"Please."

I obeyed, not because I wanted to, but because I could tell pushing would break her.

Upstairs, I tried to lose myself in the data packet for the next V9 lesson. "The Chinese Boxer Revolution." Pages of names, maps, war theory... I barely absorbed a word. My mind kept drifting toward the old photos I'd seen — the family we used to be.

Then came the shatter.

A sharp crack of glass against tile.

"Omi, what was that?"

"I'm initiating emergency protocol. Stay calm."

I bolted down the stairs two steps at a time.

The living room was empty, but the kitchen door was ajar — and behind it, chaos.

Mom was on the floor, slumped against the fridge. Her arm dangled loosely, a spent syringe rolling away from her fingers. A thin line of saliva hung from her lips. Her pupils were tiny pinpricks. A broken glass bowl lay shattered on the floor, splattered with the remnants of whatever she had dropped.

"NO. No no no— Mom!" I skidded to my knees, grabbing her face. "Omi! Where the fuck is the med-team?"

"En route. Arrival in two minutes."

I looked around. The counter. The floor. Her purse. I scrambled, scooping up the needles, the vials, flushing labels and throwing wrappers into the trash. I wasn't even thinking — just moving. Cleaning. Hiding. Erasing.

She was too strong in the daylight to be seen like this.

When the EMTs arrived, the house already smelled sterile again. "Subject unconscious, vitals shallow," one of them said.

"Possible opioid analog." They placed her on the hover-stretcher.

I rode with her. Her hand was limp in mine, all the fire drained out of her. I squeezed tighter, like I could press life back into her skin. Like if I just held her hard enough, she wouldn't be lost.

"You don't get to leave too," I pleaded. *"Not you."*

Chapter 5

THE FPM

T he sheets rasped against my skin as I shifted, stiff from the night's vigil. The faint chemical tang of antiseptic hung in the air, sharp enough to taste. The hospital lights were dimmed, casting long shadows across the linoleum floor. A half-empty bottle of water sat beside him, sweating onto the windowsill. I hadn't meant to fall asleep, but my neck ached from where it had been pressed against the edge of the hospital cot all night.

I rose slowly from the chair, rubbing the crick in my neck and letting my gaze linger on her. She was still there—still breathing.

Mom looked small, fragile. There was an IV in her arm, a monitor clipped to her finger, and an emergency patch still on her temple from when the TheraDroid team had revived her. Her once-pristine hair was tangled in pieces, and her face, always so composed, bore the cracks of pain and shame like dried clay.

She looked... human. For the first time in a long time, I saw her not as the impossibly perfect mother, the composed professional, the hologram of strength she always projected to the world. She looked like someone who had fallen hard—and who maybe had been falling for a long time.

I turned toward the window and watched a sleek med-hover pull into the docking station on the far end of the city skyline. School would be starting soon.

"I'm not going," I mumbled to no one in particular.

Omi didn't protest.

Mom stirred. My stomach cinched tight. For a moment, I thought she was slipping away, not waking up.

I turned just as her eyes flickered open. They were glassy and rimmed red. For a moment, she seemed unsure of where she was. Then she saw me. And the guilt came flooding back across her face like a broken dam.

"Maigo…" Her voice was weak, rasped from dehydration and whatever sedative they'd given her.

I was at her side in an instant. Her hand, when it found mine, was dry and brittle. The veins standing out like rivers on a drought map.

"I'm so sorry," she whispered. Her fingers trembled as she reached for my hand. "I didn't want you to see me like that."

I wanted to tell her to stop, because every word felt like a crack in something too brittle to fix. "You think I care?" I said, brushing the hair from her forehead. "You're here. That's all that matters."

She shook her head slowly. "You don't understand. I've tried so hard to protect you from all this. To be strong, to keep it all together."

"You don't have to be strong all the time," my eyes started to water. "Not for me. Not anymore."

Mom looked at me, really looked. "You've grown up so fast."

I squeezed her hand. "I think we both have some catching up to do."

A faint smile tugged at her lips.

"I've missed this," she murmured. "Just sitting here, with you."

"I was thinking about that the other day.. When I was little, you used to walk me to school every morning. Remember?"

She laughed lightly. "Even in the rain."

"You'd always wear that giant plastic poncho, like a jellyfish."

"And you'd complain the whole time."

"I wasn't complaining," I protested with a grin. "I was just... terrified. Those damn butterflies."

"Oh god, the butterflies," she laughed, wincing slightly. "You used to scream like they were combat drones chasing you or something."

"Hey! Those wings flapped with purpose."

She wiped a tear from the corner of her eye. "You always had the most dramatic imagination."

I smirked. "Maybe I was just ahead of my time. Butterfly wings. Causality. Chaos. The butterfly effect."

Mom rolled her eyes. "Don't start with the philosophy. I'm barely holding it together."

I quieted, letting the moment breathe. The beeping of the monitor filled the space between us for a while.

"You know," she said after a pause, "when you were born, we wanted to do it at home. Natural, gentle... ethereal. We had it all planned out. But you—you had other plans."

My eyes lit up. "This I haven't heard."

"My water broke two weeks early. We hadn't finished prepping for a home birth, so he loaded me into the backseat. But the hover starter failed. Maze tried for five minutes to get it working before realizing we didn't have five minutes." She laughed again, breathier this time. "So he carried me back inside—no shoes, middle of winter—and ran me up the stairs. I barely made it into the tub before you came screaming into the world." She chuckled, voice rough with memory. "I remember the sound your father's bare feet made on the icy tile — every step like a slap."

"Dad delivered me?" Although, I hadn't seen him in years that made me feel closer to him. Like he was there in the hospital for a moment.

"Hands shaking the whole time," she said. "He cried harder than I did. Danced around, carrying you in his arms."

We both laughed, and for a moment it was like the world outside the room didn't exist. Like we had stepped into a memory too sacred for time to interrupt.

The warmth between us lingered, until my expression darkened—just slightly.

"I have to ask." I was torn between preserving the moment, and addressing the elephant in the room. "Mom, what really happened to Dad?"

Her smile froze. She looked away, her eyes fixed on the far wall as if the answer were hiding there.

"Because I don't believe the official story," I added, desperately trying to lighten the mood. "Gotta do some fact-checking, here!"

Mom swallowed.

I got serious again. "I think it's time I knew the truth."

She stayed quiet for a long time. Her fingers moved across the hospital sheet in slow, anxious patterns, like she was braiding invisible strands of thought into a line she could hold onto. Outside the window, the day had fully bloomed, but the sky remained gray. Los Mitos' climate control must've been running on reduced settings again.

Then, finally, she gestured me closer and gently stroked my scalp. Her fingers wove through my hair with slow, deliberate care, each touch sparking the deep, almost-forgotten safety of childhood. "Your father was a good man," she began, softly. "Not perfect, not easy... but good. Hardworking, hard-loving. Everything he did, he did for us. He used to say there was no pain in the world he couldn't carry, so long as he knew we were okay."

I leaned closer, relaxing the urge to disrupt.

"Maze hated the way Sylvain was running things. He used to sit up late at night, pacing the kitchen floor, talking about how fast the world was changing—how it wasn't natural. How it wasn't ours anymore. I didn't understand it, not fully. I was too caught up in keeping our life clean and pretty. He saw through all that."

I pictured the kitchen light slicing through the darkness, Dad's silhouette moving back and forth like a zoo animal.

She turned my head and my gaze with a solemn, steady look. "He used to say Sylvain didn't just want control over the people. He wanted their hearts, their souls, their beliefs. He wanted to be the only thing left to worship. The only thing anyone would even think to submit to."

There was a weight in her words that pressed against my chest like a boulder.

She went back to combing my hair with her hand. "Your father believed in something bigger. Not one specific religion, necessarily. But in the right to believe. In the beauty of mystery. The importance of asking the big questions, and not having them answered by one man's logic."

I stared at her, stunned.

"He joined the FPM," she said. "The Free People's Ministry. That's what it stands for. It's not what you think—there's no violent revolution, no chaos. They're not trying to bring back the wars of the old world. They're trying to reintroduce spirituality… faith… choice. They think the soul is dying, Maigo. They're trying to save it."

"The FPM…" I echoed, the name sinking like an anchor. Part of me wanted to run straight out of the hospital, track him down, demand why he left. The other part wanted to collapse and cry like a little kid. Neither part won.

Mom continued. "He didn't want to leave. But once the regime caught wind of his involvement, things escalated. Fast. He started getting followed. They hacked our home systems. There were threats. You were just a baby." Her voice cracked. "I told him to run. I told him if he really wanted to help us… he had to disappear. Not for a few weeks. Not for months. For good. I watched the man I loved walk out the front door and never come back—just so our son could live free of fear."

I imagined the shadows clinging to our fence line. Mom living in fear. Dad desperate to protect his family. The unseen weight behind every click of the front door locking. I swallowed hard, my throat desperate for moisture. "And you've been carrying that all this time?" I whispered.

She nodded. "I didn't tell you because I didn't want you wrapped up in it. I wanted you to be normal. To focus on school, on being a kid. But that world kept closing in anyway, didn't it?"

I nodded, barely.

"I used drugs because the weight of it crushed me," Mom admitted. "I would've rather you hated me for being an addict than knowing what your father gave up to protect you." Her face twisted with emotion, and she looked away. "And now you've seen me broken in both ways."

I reached out and gently turned her face back toward me. "I don't hate you, I've been angry. I've been confused. But I never stopped loving you. You're still the person who walked me to school every day, who saved me from butterflies and packed me the weirdest lunches. You're still my mom."

She began to cry again, but this time with a kind of release. She held my hand like it was a life raft.

"I forgive you," I said. "For not telling me. For everything."

We stayed like that for a while—just breathing. Letting it all pass between us without words.

Then Mom leaned forward and wiped her eyes.

"If you ever want to know more," she said, "if you want to find the people he worked with… there's a place you can go. Quietly. Carefully."

"*What?*" I straightened. "Where?"

"It's that little place in the Inner Ring. The Japanese restaurant called 'Kyodain Tokage.' It means 'The Giant Lizard.' They make that mochi you like so much—the Dragonfire."

"I remember," I said. "We just had it with Leigh and Terra."

Lisa nodded. "Exactly. You can go there. I think you ask for the 'quiet booth in the back.' That's what Maze always called it. If someone there knows the code, they'll tell you something strange —like a joke that doesn't land. That's how you'll know."

I sat back, absorbing it all. The FPM. Dad. Sylvain's god-complex. And my mother, once a perfect image of strength, now beautifully, painfully human.

I didn't speak again until the nurse entered and began quietly checking mom's vitals.

"*Omi,*" I ordered silently, "*set a route to Kyodain Tokage.*"

"*I already anticipated your decision, Master Maigo,*" Omi replied gently. "*Shall we take the subway today? Might be good for reflection.*"

I stood up and nodded. She knew where I was going.

I kissed her on the forehead. "I'll be back soon."

She smiled without opening her eyes.

The subway platform groaned beneath the weight of the crowd. Above it, the ceiling screens played a montage of propaganda: smiling children in school uniforms, arms raised in synchronized salute; artificial trees filtering toxin-rich air; a slow fade-in of Sylvain's symbol glowing over the words:

Our World. Our Way.

I stared straight ahead, hands tucked in my jacket pockets, as the train roared into the station. Its sleek, metallic frame was still smeared with rain and graffiti. Someone had tagged one of the cars with a crude message:

WE ARE NOT MACHINES.

The words were slashed with red ink, but still visible. The doors opened with a hydraulic hiss. I stepped inside.

The train smelled like sweat and synthetic lemon cleaner, undercut with something far worse —like burned chemicals and skin. The seats were sticky with old grime. When I sat, the fabric exhaled a musty sigh, like it remembered every ghost who'd rested there before me. The lighting flickered. A broken ad panel glitched between an AI dental surgeon and a missing child report.

The car was half-full.

To my left, two figures sat side by side, rocking in a mismatched rhythm. Their eyes were sunken, fingers twitching. Augmented veins glowed faintly blue beneath their skin. They looked like they hadn't eaten in days.

On the far end of the car, a man dressed in soiled priest robes gripped a metal pole shaped like a crucifix. His collar was torn, and one of his arms had been replaced with a cheap mechanical limb wrapped in linen, as if he was ashamed of it. He was barefoot, eyes closed, muttering prayers beneath his breath. A halo had been etched crudely into the skin of his forehead—burned in by hand.

Across from me, sat a young woman with neck augments designed for harvesting atmospheric data and filtering air—illegal in most sectors now. Her coat was pulled up around her face, and she flinched every time the lights flickered, like she was being hunted.

A little boy sat down beside me.

He was maybe eight or nine. Small. Wearing an oversized sweater, torn sandals, and a knitted hat that covered most of his face. His eyes were massive and soft—too worn for someone that young. He didn't look scared. Just... stoic. "I haven't seen you on this line before," the boy said, looking up at me.

I blinked, surprised by the confidence of his voice. "I don't take it often."

"Are you lost?"

"No," I answered. "Not really."

The boy nodded like he had just figured me out. "My name's Dev."

"I'm Maigo."

"I sleep on this train," Dev said matter-of-factly. "The tunnels are the only place they won't throw us out. I know every route. Every conductor. Which seats don't have blood on them."

"That's... horrible," I murmured.

Dev shrugged. "It's the only place I'm allowed to exist. In the dark."

I looked at him carefully, and went two for two on room-filling elephants. "Where are your parents?"

Dev didn't flinch. "They told me that believing in God was a mental illness. They said if I didn't get help, I couldn't stay. So I left." He smiled. "I like it better out here, anyway. The stars are more real when you look at them with your eyes closed."

Something about his tone reminded me of the V9 simulations—when my classmates got too into it. Too convinced. But Dev wasn't playing a role.

"You really believe?" I asked. "In.. God?"

"Of course," Dev answered instantly. "That's the only reason I keep going."

"But… why live like this? Why not just say the right things? Pretend, at least?"

Dev stared forward, watching the tunnel race past the windows. His reflection flickered in and out of sight. "Because the only sin," he said slowly, "is being fake. God doesn't judge suffering. Suffering's part of the story. But being someone you're not? That kills the soul." His voice wasn't loud, but it clung to me — thin and persistent, like smoke threading its way into my lungs.

I swallowed. His words resonated too much.

Dev turned back to me with a small smile. "You'll see. If you listen real careful when you're hurting, that's when he speaks the loudest."

The train started to slow.

"This is your stop," Dev said.

I glanced out the window, confused. "How did you—"

But the boy was already gone, moving down the car with his little backpack swinging behind him.

The train stopped, announcing our arrival at "Kyodain Tokage Station."

I stepped off, suddenly uncertain whether the boy had been real at all. I looked back into the train, but the car was dark. Just flickering light. No sign of Dev.

Omi chimed in his ear with uncharacteristic gentleness. *"Are you okay, Master Maigo?"*

I nodded. *"I think I believe.. I don't know in what. But… something."*

"That's enough to begin," Omi replied. *"By the way, I don't see the value in reporting any of this. I find it to be nourishing to your adolescent development."*

My telecoms buzzed.

Incoming Call: Yoen Muse

I accepted.

Yoen's voice was sharp with excitement.

"Bro! I have a crazy story for you. You free to hang out later?"

"I'm kind of on a mission," I said.

"Ooooh, secret mission? I'm guessing that's why you skipped school today."

"Something like that."

"Alright, alright. Well, hit me later. I need you in the V9 sim tomorrow. I'll give you a rundown."

"Yeah," I said. "I'll call you when I get home."

"Bet. Talk soon, all-star." Yoen hung up.

I stepped into the station, following the familiar signs for the restaurant district. The lights above flickered between ads for hover blade upgrades and pre-mixed gene mods. The restaurant was on the other side of the street. My next step would lead me into the shadows of something older than the world I grew up in. Something sacred.

Kyodain Tokage was quieter than I expected. The bell on the door didn't ring when I stepped in—just the low chime of an ambient frequency. It was calming.

The air was warm, thick with spice and incense, faintly sweet like candied ginger left in the sun. The interior was a cluttered shrine of contradictions. Traditional paper lanterns hovered in the air beside glowing LED menus. A mechanical koi fish swam laps in a shallow marble basin beneath a bamboo faucet that dripped. On the walls: minimalist portraits of masked women, collaged beside vintage calligraphy scrolls and faded propaganda art repurposed as decor.

Behind the register I saw a woman with skin like obsidian metal, her arms a network of shimmering cybernetic tubes and chrome knuckles.

Her face was human—half, at least—the other half a modular panel of light and expression. I watched her for a moment. She took orders, processed transactions, restocked mochi trays, sorted digital payments, and played a holographic mahjong game—all at once.

I hesitated, my mouth dry. "Um..." I started, voice cracking. "Do you know anything about the... FPM?" All that smooth talk mom prepped me for went out the window.

She didn't respond. Not even a blink. Just moved a stack of trays and ran three transactions at once with her hands while swiping through documents with her eyes.

"What am I doing?" I almost turned around.

But something surfaced in my mind—an old echo. A soft voice in a warm room. My mother, humming while doing the laundry. A tune and a verse that made no sense to me then, but suddenly made all the sense in the world now.

"He stands with all, yet waits for none... He smiles at you yourself. When called upon, he breaks the phone—demanding ego death."

I whispered it, barely audible. Catching a fraction of her attention.

But the moment I said "ego death," the woman froze.

All her limbs stopped moving. The trays hovered mid-air in her magnetic field. The holo-panels dimmed. She slowly turned her head, both halves of her face now aligned with eerie precision. "Follow me," she said simply.

I followed her through the kitchen, past steaming vats of broth and two chefs who didn't look up once, as if this kind of thing happened more often than one would think.

A narrow staircase led downward—wooden steps, darkened from age and smoke. As we descended, the air thickened with the scent of burning resin and something older. The scent of earth that hadn't seen light in decades.

At the bottom, the woman bowed without a word and returned upstairs.

I stood in a dim corridor lit by a single strip of neon light above a rusted iron door. I opened it.

Inside was a chamber that felt older than the world.

The room was split directly down the center. On one side: stone floors, hand-chiseled with ancient symbols. Walls of rough clay and woven tapestries. Candles flickered in sacred patterns. Sculptures of kin or deities—*I couldn't tell which*—sat in meditative poses beneath slow-turning fans made of real feathered leaves.

On the other side: carbon fiber panels with an iridescent sheen. Monitors flickering with live satellite data. Energy weapons stacked in racks beside scrolls. The air buzzed with electric hums. A row of books—some paper, some digital—lined a high shelf beneath tactical gear and neuro-calibration helmets.

I felt like I was standing between two worlds. And on either side, seated in silent meditation, were two towering men. Identical in build. Identical in face.

The twin on the left wore flowing white robes. His hair tied in a topknot. His eyes were closed, mouth relaxed in an almost musical smile.

The twin on the right wore matte black militant armor—tactical boots, data bracers, and a sleek rifle laid beside him like a pet dog at rest. He, too, sat cross-legged. Eyes closed. Arms on his knees.

Before I could speak, the robed one opened his eyes with casual brightness.

"Oh, I thought that was you, Maigo," he said, grinning.

The militant opened his eyes next. "You've grown up so much, kid," he added, in a voice that was firmer, but kind. "I'm Bolt, and that's my brother Ino."

"I—" I stammered. "Are you the FP—?"

"If you're looking for your father," Ino said with a chuckle, "you've just missed him."

"Don't listen to that fool," Bolt interjected. "Maze has been out of the country for almost two years."

I stepped further into the chamber, trying to find something to say. "My mom told me. About him. About what he did. I guess I'm here because… I want to understand."

The brothers looked at me with unblinking patience.

"I want to join the FPM," I exclaimed.

Ino burst into laughter. A deep, musical laugh that bounced between the stone walls. "You don't ask how to be free, you just are," he said, wiping a tear from his eye.

Bolt stood slowly and crossed his arms. "Sorry, kid. Maze would never allow it. You've got too much heat on you. And you're marked. V9."

"I didn't ask to be marked," I snapped. "I didn't ask for any of this."

The room went quiet again. I waited for a reply I didn't get.

"I'm supposed to be part of the summer program," I continued, voice cracking slightly. "They're sending me deeper into V9. That simulation shit. The ones that break people. I feel like… like I'm betraying my father. Like I'm part of the machine he tried to fight."

Neither brother said anything. Their silence broke me.

"I'm so fucking lost," I admitted. "And I'm so tired of pretending I'm not. So... what do I do?"

Ino stood as well, mirroring his twin. They began to speak—separately, but together. Their words layered into a single thread of meaning.

"Things are always simple," said Ino.

"For complicated people," Bolt followed.

"There is always a choice to be made."

"And a path laid out ahead."

"Mistakes should be learning," said Ino.

"Not leaning," Bolt disrupted. "Every moment is part of you."

Then together, they said in unison "to love yourself is to be free."

The chamber fell silent. I felt the natural conclusion of our conversation.

The brothers closed their eyes again, and returned to meditation. Their hums echoed through the chamber like the slow turning of planets.

I turned back toward the tunnel. I didn't understand everything I'd heard, but the ache in my chest loosened. Just enough to breathe again.

I walked back up into the world of light. Their voices weren't loud, but they clung to me — thin and persistent, like smoke threading its way into my lungs.

A text from mom rerouted me home, instead of the hospital:

"Why don't you just head home tonight? I'll get discharged in the morning and I want you to make it to school. Love you."

Chapter 6

TERRA'S TUNDRA

I could feel the frost before I even entered the simulation.

Not real frost, of course—but something colder. A silence layered in guilt and unspoken things. The kind that settles between two people who once meant everything to each other... and now look away like strangers on a train.

Even the air in the V9 classroom felt off—dense, smothering, thick. Like a weighted blanket.

Terra sat three seats away from me, her eyes fixed forward, lips sealed, arms crossed tight like she was holding something in. Frozen in a defensive position.

I didn't blame her. I just didn't know what to do with the blame. It was too soon to forgive myself, and too late to make a better choice. It was the type of thing I just had to deal with.

The terminals hummed low, barely audible beneath the screaming silence of the room. The V9 pods stood in their neat little rows, glinting beneath the sterile glow of the ceiling lights, like Venus Fly Traps waiting for volunteers. This would be the place where I learned how to take a life. The place where I watched my friends become monsters. No place for empathy. A place for violence. Moral suicide. An evil sickness that would soon be given to children across the world. I hated myself for being part of it.

Omi adjusted the screen on my telecoms implant, projecting my vital data into the empty space above my desk. Heart rate slightly elevated. Temperature normal. Mental focus: declining. *"Are you feeling alright, Master Maigo?"*

"I'm fine," I lied. *"Just… cold."*

"Ah, the nerves before a big test. I'm sure you'll do great!" Omi replied. *"Shall I play the jungle drums of confidence?"*

"No." I flexed my fingers against the desk, trying to chase away the stiffness creeping up my arms.

Yoen wasn't in yet. I guessed he'd be late. But last night he picked up when I called, right after I got home from the restaurant. He was already two bowls deep in noodle soup, talking my ear off about how "we got cooked" in the Chinese Boxing Revolution sim.

"Straight-up chaos," he had said between slurps. "Jace tried to lead a protest and got lynched by the townspeople. Dude stuttered like a broken bot at the podium. Luna tried to blow up a rail line— ended up blowing herself up. Terra? Wouldn't stop complaining about you. Wouldn't even chase the objective. Cobb looked ready to throw a chair through a window."

I remember being quiet for a second, unsure whether to be disappointed in them or ashamed of myself. "What's next?" I asked.

"Internment camp," Yoen answered with a grin I could hear through the line. "WW2 era. Soviet Russia. Straight-up frozen hellscape. You, Terra, Luna, and Max are prisoners. The rest of us are Red Army. Our job's to keep you locked up. No mercy."

I'd hung up after that, feeling like I'd already failed whatever test was waiting for me.

Dr. Cobb stormed in, Light trailing two paces behind. The door hissed shut with a finality that made the air thicken even more. Cobb's untucked Sylvain pendant bounced against his chest with every step—brazen, unbothered. His eyes scanned the room, not taking attendance so much as weighing us like produce.

"Good morning, initiates," he said, his voice a thin blade hidden in a silk glove. "Today marks your final simulation of the spring term."

The temperature in the room dropped another degree. Or maybe that was just me.

"This scenario will test every ounce of what you've learned so far. It will strip you of safety, rank, and warmth. It will force you to bleed, to break, and rebuild yourselves in the image we require. Some of you will suffer. Some of you may die." A small smile tugged at the corner of his mouth. "And all of you will be watched."

I noticed Light grimace softly beside him. Cobb caught it and grinned wider.

Light stepped up next, his lack of charisma overwritten by the importance of his words. "As you know, the summer term of V9 is new. But it will become tradition. The students who qualify gain access to the highest-level diplomatic and technological programs. Some may lead peace initiatives. Others will find themselves in high-ranking political offices. And the best among you..." He paused. "The architects of the future."

I clenched my fists so tightly my nails bit my palms. That word—*architects*. That was Sylvain's word.

Cobb sweetened the pot. "You'll receive real-world certifications. A monthly government stipend. Your families moved onto the preferred citizenry track. This isn't just a reward. It's your legacy."

Legacy.

I thought of the boy on the train. *"Eight years old. Proud of his suffering. Sleeping underground because the surface world had no room for belief. What legacy did he have?"* I hung my head in shame. *"None. He was too pure for this place. And me? I was still here. Still nodding along. Still pretending I hadn't already broken something inside myself just to survive."*

Cobb wasn't finished. "This isn't about passing or failing anymore. This is about proving your loyalty to the world we're building. A world without chaos. Without myth. Without lies."

I felt my pulse ticking against my jaw.

Without hope. Without faith.

On the other end of the table, Terra shifted slightly in her chair. She didn't look at me. Not once. I used to be the only thing that could pull her out of a spiral. Now, I wasn't even a ripple in her tide.

The last time we'd spoken, she threw a little girl into a death stream and didn't even flinch. I wondered if she was bothered by their speech the same way I was. I'd always known her to be a bit rebellious, but there was more to it than that.

Something that reminded me of me. She was always carving space to be herself. Forcing the world around her to accept her entirety. And yet, here we were—both still chasing approval from a system that rewarded silence and obedience more than truth.

"Suit up," Cobb said, his voice almost bored now. "And remember... victory is only half the mission. We're looking for cognition. Alignment. Loyalty. Good luck!"

"Alignment." That word hit like an unseen shove. I stood, legs heavier than they should've been, and walked toward my pod. Part of me screamed to turn around. To tear the pod apart. To run.

But I was already moving. Drawn into my fate like magnetic poles.

The pod's lid clamped shut around me. A hiss of vacuum seals. A click of brain interface needles finding their marks.

I stood in a line of hollow bodies, boots cracking against frostbitten mud, waiting for a bowl of soup that barely counted as edible. The wind carried the smell of rust and smoke from the copper mines, sweeping over the camp like a reminder that the earth itself hated us. Everything hurt—my fingers, my ears, the cartilage in my nose. Even my thoughts felt brittle, like they'd snap if I thought too hard about how long I'd been shivering.

Someone behind me leaned in. His voice was so dry it sounded brittle. "New here, huh?"

I turned.

A man with a jagged jawline and haunted eyes met my gaze. His cap was military surplus, tilted low enough to shade whatever he didn't want me to see.

"Yeah," I said. "Just visiting."

He chuckled—a sound so hollow it barely counted as a laugh. "Anton," he said.

"Maigo."

We shuffled forward.

The man two places ahead of us collapsed, soup spilling out of his hands. Nobody helped. A guard dragged him away like you'd move a sack of wet trash.

The line closed without breaking stride.

When we got our soup—if you could call it that—we found a place on a rotting bench under a tin awning. Our breath rose like smoke signals from dying villages.

Anton pointed through the fog. "See that tower? Old communications rig. Dead now. But there's a tunnel beneath it. Real long one."

I said nothing. Just sipped the broth, letting it burn my cracked lips.

He kept talking. "I used to fix the power grids. Before. Had a boy. Eight years old. Tough little thing. Carried a satchel everywhere like it was armor. When the soldiers came, I told him to hide." His hand shook. Soup sloshed onto his coat. "I never found him." He didn't cry. He didn't even blink. "I've been mapping this place for months. Rotations, blind spots, guard habits. I know how to get out. I just need… one more." He stared at me, through me.

"You sure you can trust me?" I asked.

"No."

"But you're asking anyway."

He nodded once. A soldier's nod. "Hope's heavier than suspicion. And I'm fresh out of both."

I could feel the chains of the simulation tightening, trying to crush that flicker of rebellion. I didn't care.

"I'm in," I said.

We finished eating in silence, the cold gnawing through the last thin walls between us and whatever came next.

They herded us into cargo trucks with no windows and dropped us at the edge of the mines — a chasm in the tundra that looked less dug and more torn open by violence.

I followed the line of men down the black slope, boots slipping in the powdered ice. The deeper we went, the more the air thickened—like breathing through wet cement. Every breath carved new wounds inside my chest. Sparks spit sideways from pickaxes hitting mineral veins. Echoes rebounded wildly, making it impossible to tell where the real danger was.

Somewhere in that noise, I spotted Max.

He was almost unrecognizable —
straighter, heavier somehow, like the gravity here
pressed him differently. His face was a smear of
dust and blood, but his eyes burned the way they
always did: like he was daring the world to come at
him first.

I slipped into line beside him. "Max," I
whispered. "I need to tell you something."

He didn't stop chipping. His axe rose and
fell with a dead rhythm.

"There's a guy. Anton. He's planning an
escape. Real plan. Tonight."

Max froze just a beat too long. "Who else
knows?"

"Nobody."

"We need the girls too."

"Luna. Terra."

Max's jaw flexed. He nodded once.

The scarred man on my left—more bone
than flesh—leaned into our breath cloud. "Latrine
rotation between quarters," he rasped. "You bribe
the guard, you get through. They don't pay them
enough to ask questions."

Before I could thank him, a voice cracked through the tunnel like a rifle shot.

"You three. Eyes front." A guard stomped toward us, swinging his baton in lazy circles like a vulture testing its wings.

Max straightened. "I was asking about his pickaxe grip, sir."

The guard stopped in front of me. "Is that right, piglet?"

I nodded.

The guard's gaze shifted to the informant. His smile was slow and ugly.

"And what about this little worm? He doesn't look like a grip expert."

The scarred man paled. "I—I was just—"

"He was listening in," Max interrupted, voice flat. "We told him to move."

The guard didn't hesitate. The first strike broke something deep — you could hear it over the hammering picks. The second knocked the man's breath out. The third folded him. The fourth cracked his skull open against the stone wall. He dropped like a sack of bones and dust.

Nobody moved.

Nobody reacted.

The guard wiped his nose with his glove, gave Max a nod, and sauntered away.

I stared at the cracked earth where the man had fallen, feeling something primal and ugly knot up inside my ribs.

We finished the shift in dead silence.

I didn't look at Max. I didn't want him to see that somewhere deep down, a small part of me thought, *this is what survival costs.*

By the time we got back to the men's quarters, the sun had died and the real cold had begun. It seeped into our bones as we slid into our bunks, quiet, bruised, and waiting for nightfall.

We waited until the bells rang twice— once for lights out, and once to signal the beginning of the guard rotation. That gave us twenty minutes.

Anton took the lead. "We'll need a pouch. Something with bite."

"Who has one?" Max asked, still rubbing the dirt from his knuckles.

Anton scanned the dorm. He pointed with his chin. "That guy. Thin one. Keeps his tucked in his boot. Doesn't have the brawn to say no."

I didn't want to do it.

But I did it anyway.

I cornered the guy at the edge of the bunk stacks with Max shadowing me. His eyes darted between us, panicked and twitching.

"Hey," I said, voice low. "We need your tobacco."

He clutched his boot like it was his last possession on Earth. "Please, it's all I have left." It was.

Max stepped closer. "And we need it more."

He looked at us like we were monsters. I felt like one.

He didn't fight. Just pulled it out and held it like an offering. I could see the veins in his arm throbbing, like his body knew what this moment meant.

Anton snatched it and tucked it into his coat.

When the guard finally came to do the headcount, we waited until he passed our bunk. Anton stood and casually let the pouch dangle between two fingers.

The guard paused. Eyes narrowed. "What's that?"

"A trade," Anton replied. "If you've got the spine."

The guard raised an eyebrow.

"We want in on the girls' dorm tonight," I said, trying to sound cocky, filthy. "You know... warm bodies, hands."

The guard's lip curled into a grin. "You think I haven't thought about it?" He lowered his voice. "That dorm's got a few sweet ones."

"We'll share," Max added. "But only if you play nice."

The guard's eyes darted down the hall, then back at us. "Come."

He led us through the frozen corridor, down a side path of the camp, and into the women's quarters. The smell of mildew and old sweat hit immediately—so different from the men's side only in that the silence felt worse.

We slipped through the rows of sleeping bodies and found Luna first, then Terra. Their eyes widened when they saw me.

"We're getting out," I whispered.

Luna grinned instantly. Terra looked stunned, hesitant.

Anton pressed a finger to his lips. "We've got ten minutes, maybe less."

The guard brought us to a tool shed just outside the dorm—thin wooden walls, an old barrel stove in the corner, and thick film of dust.

"I'll keep watch," he grinned. "You do your thing."

As the door closed, Luna grabbed my arm. "What's the plan?"

I looked at the walls, thin enough to hear every breath. "We make noise. Loud, stupid, believable noise."

Luna caught on immediately. "Got it." She shoved me playfully into the wall and moaned so loud it startled even me.

I slapped the boards behind her and added my own, exaggerated grunts.

"Oh my god, yes," she moaned again.

I saw Terra turn away. She didn't have to say anything. A second later, she grabbed Max by the arm and dragged him to the opposite corner.

Now there were two performances. Competing ones.

Moans, smacks, exaggerated gasps and laughter. A farce. A symphony of cruelty disguised as pleasure. The whole shed was vibrating with it. It made my stomach turn.

We kept it going for what felt like forever, until finally the door creaked open again.

The guard stepped in. "Alright stallions, it's my turn." His voice was like grease on tile. He looked at me and smirked. "Which one?"

Luna looked down.

Terra's face twisted in horror. She stepped back, hitting the wall behind her.

Time slowed.

A memory flashed in my head—Luna's voice from the ride to Josie's, telling me about the night it happened. How she'd screamed, how no one came. How she stopped believing anyone ever would.

I looked at her. Then at Terra.

I hated that I had to choose.

"That one." I pointed at Terra.

Her eyes burned into me like molten glass.

The guard grinned, stepping toward her as he began undoing his belt.

"No," she whispered.

He grabbed her by the wrist.

I started moving, but Max was already behind him.

Crack!

The shovel connected with the side of the guard's head. He dropped like a stone, face first into the cold dirt floor.

We all stood there for a second, breathing hard. Terra looked at Max like he'd just saved her life. Because he had.

Anton didn't hesitate. He stripped the guard's uniform off him, down to his thermals, and started putting it on piece by piece.

"I'll do the talking," he said. "You just follow me and stay quiet."

We dragged the body into the darkest corner and covered it with a canvas tarp. Then we stepped into the night.

The wind howled against the forest line, and the frost cracked beneath our boots. At the outer gate, a tall guard stood beneath a yellow halogen light, rifle tucked under one arm.

Anton walked right up and gave him a wink. They talked for a while in Russian, almost like old friends reliving 'the good old days.' The guard smiled and laughed for 2 minutes straight, then waved us through.

Just like that, we were outside.

Too easy.

We pushed into the forest. The trees were skeletal and reaching, and the ground was uneven and coated in thick crusts of snow. In the distance, we could see the old tower, just a black shape against a dark snow-filled sky.

Then we heard it.

The barking.

Low. Deep. Carving its way through the trees like thunder trying to speak.

Caucasian mountain dogs. The ones I'd seen sleeping in cages earlier.

The barking grew louder.

We ran like shadows fleeing the flame.

Branches clawed at our faces and coats as we pushed deeper into the forest, lungs frozen solid, legs threatening collapse. The snow dragged at our boots like hands from the earth trying to pull us under. But the barking—those deep, guttural bellows—was louder than the pain. Louder than the panic.

Luna stumbled and cried out. Her leg twisted and gave, and she crumpled face-first into the snow.

"Luna!" I dropped beside her, digging her out. Her ankle was already swelling, her eyes swelling to match.

Terra was on her knees beside us in an instant. "She can't run."

"We don't have time for this," Max hissed, turning to Anton. "What now?"

Anton scanned the tree line. A glow was coming toward us. Lanterns—two of them. The dogs sounded closer. Much closer.

"We split up," Anton ordered. "Now. I'll draw some of them away. You head for the storm hatch. It's buried just south of the tower's base. You'll see the pipe next to it."

He took the lantern with him. "Hurry. I'll hold it open."

Then he was gone, vanishing into the distance like he'd never been there.

I slung Luna's arm around my shoulders, and Terra did the same on the other side. The moon lit the base of the tower in the distance. Our only directional guidance in the blizzard. Together, we carried her forward through the drifts, moving as fast as three broken bodies could. My heart was pounding. My ears were filled with ice.

Suddenly, Luna collapsed into me entirely —offsetting my balance.

And I heard a combative growl.

I turned.

Terra was on the ground, pinned beneath a dog the size of a bear. Its thick coat was mottled with frost and blood, and its eyes were glowing with wild instinct. She was screaming—screaming my name—and kicking at the thing with everything she had. Her arms thrashed, her fists beat its back, but it didn't move.

"Maigo!" she cried. "Maigo, help me!"

I moved toward her. Then stopped.

I looked back at Luna—barely conscious, bleeding, unable to walk. I looked at Terra again, now half-buried in snow as the dog's teeth tore through her sleeve.

I couldn't save them both.

I knew that.

But I didn't move.

My mind tried to calculate, to rationalize. What were the odds? What was the risk? Who could I still save? What did this mean for the mission?

And then she looked at me—right into my soul—and whispered, "I love you."

The dog lunged, jaws snapping shut around her neck. The sound it made—wet, raw, final—broke something in me.

She didn't scream after that.

The dog began to shake her like a chew toy, slamming her body into the ground again and again, until the snow around them turned pink.

I couldn't breathe.

I dragged Luna forward, head down, vision tunneling. I saw Anton ahead, maybe seventy, eighty feet away, holding a rusted hatch open at the forest's edge, lantern flickering.

"Move, Maigo!" he shouted.

I didn't look back. I couldn't.

We dove inside just as the next set of barking broke through the trees behind us. Anton slammed the hatch closed, bolting it shut. There was a sliver of light beaming through a crack—but the snow came fast, pouring down over it, snuffing it out. Everything went black.

I sat in that darkness, my breath ragged, my body shaking from more than cold. "She said she loved me," I muttered.

Luna leaned into me, her head resting on my shoulder, arms wrapped tight around her chest. Her cheek brushed my jaw. "She made a choice," she whispered.

"No," I said, barely audible. "I did."

We were safe . The dogs couldn't find us there. The soldiers wouldn't look that deep in a storm. But I couldn't stop hearing her voice— begging, pleading, believing I'd come for her.

And I hadn't.

I closed my eyes. And somewhere in the blizzard above, a girl I loved was being swallowed by the forest.

I didn't sleep.

The storm howled like a banshee just beyond the metal skin of our shelter. We were buried alive, waiting out a war of elements.

Anton had drifted off near the far wall, curled like a child, drooling and mumbling in his native tongue.

Luna hadn't stopped shivering. She stayed pressed against me for warmth, chin tucked into my chest, breath steaming through my shirt.

"You okay?" I finally asked, though I already knew the answer.

She pulled her knees tighter to her chest. "I think so." Her voice was steady—too steady.

She was waiting. I could feel it.

"Terra," she said eventually, like she was tasting the word for poison.

I didn't answer.

"She said she loved you," Luna continued. "Right before she died. That's… kind of pathetic, don't you think?"

I flinched at the glitch in her performance.

She looked up at me, searching my eyes, but I kept them fixed on the condensation gathering on the wall. "I mean the timing was really desperate," Luna said, softer now. "She thought you'd save her just because she said that. She didn't mean it."

"She was fighting for her life," I said.

"Exactly. And you chose me." Luna leaned closer. "You didn't have to. No one forced you. You made the choice, Maigo."

That's what you think this is? I stayed quiet.

Luna held firm, awaiting a response.

"You didn't hear her the way I did," I finally said. "The panic. The fear in her voice."

"She was always dramatic," Luna whispered. "That doesn't make it real."

What the hell kind of person says that?

I looked down at her. Her eyes were wide, sweet, like a deer. Calculated. She smiled as if this entire moment was some kind of shared victory.

But it wasn't.

I didn't feel victorious. I felt sick.

"You okay?" she asked, brushing her hand along my jaw.

I nodded. Lied.

She kissed me—slow, almost reverent. Her lips were soft, but something about it felt... off. Like I was being sealed into a contract I didn't remember signing.

"You'll stay close after this, right?" she whispered.

I didn't answer. She didn't seem to need one.

We emerged from the storm shelter just after dawn. The forest looked like a photograph—silent, empty, frozen in time. You'd never guess what had happened there the night before.

The three of us trudged back toward the rendezvous point—the edge of the base, where the simulation's invisible wall hummed faintly beneath the trees.

And waiting for us, as if summoned by our grief, was Doctor Cobb. He stood there with his arms behind his back, flanked by holographic stats and playback footage of our entire simulation. His smile was the kind you'd see on a man handing out awards at a hospice.

"Well done," he said. "All three of you— excellent performance."

I stared at him. Luna shifted uncomfortably beside me.

"I want to commend you, Maigo," Cobb said. "You, in particular, showed unwavering commitment to the objective. You made hard choices. You let emotion exist where it needed to, but you never let it disrupt the mission. Not when you allowed a fellow prisoner to be beaten for your silence. Not when you manipulated a naive guard. And certainly not when Terra fell behind."

My stomach turned. He kept going.

"It was beautiful," Cobb said. "You saw the bigger picture. And you never forgot the objective. That's what we're looking for in a recruit."

"Objective? Fell behind? Beautiful?" I wanted to rip the words out of his mouth.

He turned to Luna. "And you, Miss Grey. Impressive resilience. I expected nothing less."

Then to Max, who looked even more disgusted than I did. "The rest of your classmates didn't fare as well," Cobb said. "Which is why those who are eligible will receive a telecoms message shortly."

And just like that, he tapped a button, and the world blinked out.

Back in the classroom, the hum of the chests faded. The lights overhead returned to their normal, sterile white.

Everyone sat in stunned silence, waiting. Recovering.

Then the telecoms began pinging, one by one.

Yoen's face lit up. "Fuck yeah!" he whispered.

Jade followed soon after.

Jace debated with Doctor Cobb after receiving his rejection letter.

I didn't even look. I already knew.

Across the room, Terra's chest sat unopened.

Doctor Light noticed me staring at it. "Don't worry. When cortisol and adrenaline levels reach a certain peak, we have to do a longer recovery process. Terra will be just fine."

Luna was watching me, eyes soft, lips curved. When class was dismissed, she lingered. "Hey," she said, brushing her fingers along my arm. "Wanna come over? I'll cook something. We could… just talk."

I hesitated.

For a moment, I thought about saying yes. About pretending none of this mattered. About burying everything I'd felt under whatever comfort she was offering.

But I couldn't.

"Not tonight," I said.

Her face barely changed, but I felt it. The fracture. Another crack in the performance.

"Oh," she said, rebooting her smile. "Okay." She kissed me—cool, controlled, careful.

"I'll call you?" I lied.

She nodded. "Sure."

And then she walked away.

I sat back down at my desk, eyes fixed on the blank wall across the room, feeling like I had just survived something far worse than a Russian winter.

Chapter 7

MAIGO'S REBIRTH

When I got home, I felt exposed. Like I was trapped in glass, being watched and judged. The weight of what happened in the last simulation was still pressing against my ribs. I could still hear Terra's voice, the terror in it. I could still see the white flash of the dog's teeth, the blood on the snow, her body going limp in the dark.

The lock clicked behind me as I stepped inside. The air smelled faintly of warm rice and citrus cleaner—comforting, familiar. And then I heard her.

"Hey, honey," Mom called from the kitchen. She stepped out with a cup of tea in her hand, her robe perfectly tied, her hair full and curled, her skin bright again. The woman in front of me was unshaken. Undeniable. Whole again.

"Hi mom," I said.

She caught it right away. That tiny weight in my voice. That pause.

Her expression softened. "Come here, Maigo."

I didn't realize how badly I needed to be held until her arms wrapped around me. I unconsciously melted into her. The dam in my tear ducts broke. My breath hitched, and for a moment I forgot how to stand on my own.

She guided me to the couch, set the tea down, and held me the way she used to when I was a kid waking from nightmares. We didn't speak right away. I was afraid if I opened my mouth, all the horrors would spill out.

But eventually I found the words. "It's… it's starting to fuck with me."

She didn't blink. She just nodded.

"These simulations—V9—it's not just training. It's not just history. They're making us into something. And I don't know who I'm becoming."

"Tell me everything," she said.

I started from the beginning of the last simulation. Every brutal detail. I told her about the escape plan. About the guard. About Terra. The sound of her begging. The way Luna clung to me afterward. The silence that came next. And then… Colonel Haines.

"She blackmailed me," I said. "She used the sewer incident against me. Told me I had no choice. Said if I didn't sign on, she'd get me and my friends in trouble. But Mom, none of it feels right. I feel like I've been walking a path that isn't meant for me."

She listened without flinching. Her eyes were glassy, but she didn't cry. I realized then that she already knew more than she ever let on. "I'm so sorry, Maigo," she whispered. "I should've told you sooner. About your father. About the truth of this world. About why he left."

"I'm not mad," I said. "I just… I don't want to lie to myself anymore. I want to feel comfortable with who I am, no matter what or who I'm around. You know.. True honesty with myself and everybody else."

She ran her fingers through my hair, brushing back the knots stress had tied. "Then let's do something honest tonight."

"What do you mean?"

"No secrets. No pretense. Just something good for our hearts." She smiled like she had a plan.

I followed her out the door without question.

We drove for miles, leaving the city's borders and venturing deep into the countryside. For a long time, there was nothing but barren desert. An endless stretch of light brown, contrasting the cloudless ocean above. I couldn't tell you what we talked about, but I remember laughing until my chest hurt. Mom had never been so funny before. After an eternity, but before sunset, we reached a giant traveling circus that had set up in the middle of nowhere. There were more hovers than I could count.

"How did you know this was here?" I asked.

"A long time ago, your father took me on a date here. Your father wasn't a timely man, so I never got the chance to ride any rides. We'd arrived just barely in time to see the main event. We were just getting to know each other and I had no idea what Maze was into, but I remember telling him I was sad that day. An hour and a half later, we were here. By the time it was over, I couldn't even remember what I was upset about. I hope it works on you."

"Do we have time to ride the rides?" I was so excited.

"Nope, the main event starts in ten minutes." She disappointed. "Let's go get our seats."

The acrobat arena was a glowing marvel. A full circle theater with floating platforms, sky-high holograms, and almost a thousand eager spectators. The show had just started when we took our seats. Front and center. Everything was motion and music. A holographic world phased into existence as the sun drifted asleep. The cast of performers, human and droid alike, took the stage.

Omi projected the holo-image of himself into a nearby empty seat, eating popcorn. *"Oh goodness, I'm excited!"*

A chrome-plated droid sprinted across a tightrope that bent and buckled under his weight, flipping mid-run before catching himself on one arm. The crowd gasped. Somewhere to the left, a woman in green synthetic silks spiraled down an invisible wire, twisting with impossible grace before locking her limbs and freezing mid-air.

Omi clapped like a child, bouncing up and down in the seat. *"How marvelous!"* He was almost as entertaining as the show.

Then a trio of performers—augmented humans with spring-loaded legs and glowing chest-cores—launched from opposite ends of the stadium, met in mid-air with a pinwheel collision, and ricocheted off each other like a firework exploding in slow motion.

Omi's holo shot out into the air, joining the pogo-men in an aerial dance. *"Look at me, Master Maigo!"*

A gust of wind from a camera drone brushed my face. I didn't realize how tightly I'd been gripping my seat until my fingers started to ache.

"This is incredible," I breathed.

But Mom just shook her head. "Wait. This is the best part."

Omi retracted his holo, sensing the seriousness of the finale.

The lights dimmed. The music softened to a piano—something warm and sad and full of longing. A single spotlight found a small figure kneeling at the center of the stage. A girl, maybe eight or nine, surrounded by an intricate web of cables like the threads of some colossal loom.

High above her, suspended from a rotating platform, were two wings—pristine, white, mechanical. They shimmered like they'd been forged from light itself.

The little girl began to climb.

Each step was careful. Deliberate. Her tiny feet danced along the lines, balancing between the chaos of wires. At one point she slipped— deliberately—but caught herself, drawing a shocked gasp from the crowd.

When she reached the top, she strapped the wings to her back. The piano swelled. Dozens of performers re-entered the arena on ropes, wires, and wings. The girl jumped.

She flew.

A perfect arc, above it all. She spun slowly, arms out, glitter falling from her palms like blessings. When she finally landed, the audience erupted in tears and cheers. My mother had both.

"She made it," I whispered.

"She always does," Mom said.

We sat in the echo of applause, and I turned to her.

"Was that… was that supposed to mean something?"

She nodded. "Every performance represents something different. But that one…" She smiled at the empty air where the girl had flown. "That's life. All of it. The maze, the climb, the stumble, the wings. And the girl—she's all of us. Pushing through a world that never makes it easy. But if you keep going, you reach something bigger than yourself."

I stared at her for a long time. At this woman I'd seen weak, shattered, perfect, and whole. Maybe I hadn't lost her after all.

"Thank you, Mom. I mean it."

"You'll be okay," she said, holding my hand. "You always have been."

Right as the performers started bowing, my telecoms buzzed.

Incoming Call: Jade

My heart sank. Jade never called me.

"Maigo," she said as soon as I answered. "It's Terra. She's in the hospital. They said it was a suicide attempt. You need to go there now."

Everything in me stopped healing. The colors around me lost their shine.

"I'm on my way."

Hospitals have a strange kind of quiet. It's not the kind that lets you focus, or the kind that begs to be broken—it's the kind that presses against your skin and makes your own breath sound too loud. I walked through it like it might shatter beneath my shoes.

She was on the fourth floor. Behind a pane of glass, Terra lay small in a wide bed. The blanket was pulled up to her chest, her arms motionless on either side, and a narrow sensor array blinked steadily across her wrist. Her hair was messy, wild in places, and the makeup she always wore had been wiped away, leaving only her.

"He'll let you see her." Omi assured me.

Her father sat in a chair beside her, his head buried in his hands.

He looked like a statue chipped from heartbreak. I stood there, frozen on the other side of the glass, not sure if I belonged here. Not sure if I hadn't helped push her to that edge.

Leigh Waters lifted his head and looked at me. His eyes were bloodshot, hollowed out in grief. We stared at each other for a long time. Then, without a word, he stood, walked to the door, and cracked it open.

"You've got five minutes," he said, voice rough. "She could use a friend." He didn't wait for me to answer. Just stepped past me and disappeared down the corridor, leaving the door open behind him.

I hesitated for a moment, afraid that I'd make things worse, then stepped inside.

Terra didn't look at me right away. Her eyes were fixed on the ceiling. There were small

specks of dried tears seasoning her cheeks, and her lips were chapped, pale. I stood at the foot of her bed, unsure how to breathe, let alone speak.

"Should I say sorry? That I'm glad she's alive? Should I tell her I love her?"

But then she spoke. "I couldn't stop seeing it." Her voice was hoarse but clear. "That dog. The way it grabbed me. The way you looked at me—like you were already mourning. I felt myself die a hundred times in my mind before I even got home."

I moved closer, slowly. Sat down in the chair Leigh had left behind.

"I didn't know where else to put the pain," she continued. "So I tried to bury it. But it was like digging a hole in my own chest. When I saw you with Luna, I… it just slammed everything on top of me all at once. Like I was being buried alive. I couldn't breathe anymore." She finally turned to look at me. Her eyes were dark, moist and cracked open like an untreated basement. "Everyone thinks I'm perfect, you know? Confident. Strong. Unshakable." She let out a brittle laugh. "But that's a lie I tell the world so I don't have to admit how scared I am of not being enough."

Something about it hit me harder than I expected. It was like watching a mirror pull back and reveal my mother.

I opened my mouth to speak, but she shook her head.

"Don't apologize," she said. "You don't owe me that. I get it now... about Luna. I was pushing you away. It scared me, being close to you. Really close. That night before everything happened—I wanted so badly to just fall into you. But I held back. I thought... if I gave you all of me and you didn't want it, I'd fall apart."

I swallowed. Hard. I thought about the little boy on the train calling inauthenticity a sin. Then everything clicked for me.

"Luna hides who she is. Masks it with beauty and bravado, like she's playing a part in someone else's story. And now I see it... and I don't like what I see."

Terra's eyes stayed on mine, waiting.

"But I saw your mask too," I said. "And I loved every broken, scared, angry, beautiful piece of you underneath it. Even the part of you that threw that little girl into the river." I paused, choking on the memory. "Even that."

The tears came quietly down her face. Not violent. Just... honest.

"I don't know when I'll get to see you again," I said. "So there's something I need to tell you."

I hesitated. She blinked, waiting.

"Sometimes I have beggar thoughts," I said. "I think about God. About what all this is for. About who I'm supposed to become."

She nodded slowly, still silent.

"My dad... he's alive. He's part of a group that's fighting to bring belief back into the world. Real belief. Not control. Not worship. Just the freedom to feel something greater than this mess. I've been recruited into the V9 summer program and—honestly—it feels like I'm betraying everything he stood for. Everything I stand for."

Terra reached out, rested her fingers on the back of my hand. Her grip was weak, but it was hers. "No matter what you do," she said gently, "just make sure you're still you when you do it."

That was when Leigh returned. His voice was low, but firm. "Time's up."

"*Say it Master Maigo!*" Omi dared. "*You may not get another chance.*"

I stood. I didn't want to go. I looked at her one last time. The words were right there. "*I love you.*" But I couldn't say them. Not yet. Not like this. So I just nodded. Let my hand linger against hers a moment longer.

Then I left.

There was a strange hover parked in our driveway.

It wasn't the polished corporate kind or the sleek personal models that lined our neighborhood streets. This one was a rusted green, with dense framing, like it had driven through warzones and never bothered to get cleaned up. The windshield had a spider crack in the top-left corner. Two small flags—one white, one black—fluttered on the antenna.

And on the patio-deck, in full meditative pose, sat Bolt.

He was perched perfectly still, cross-legged on one of our garden chairs like it was a throne. A thermos steamed at his side, fingers pressed together, eyes closed.

"Hey, kid! How've you been?" he said suddenly, before he opened his eyes.

I stepped onto the porch. "You have to teach me how you guys do that."

He cracked one eye open and smirked. "That's top secret."

Before I could ask why he was there, Mom walked past us on her way inside, holding a bag of groceries like this was just another Tuesday.

"Evening, Bolt," she said casually.

"Lisa," he greeted with a nod.

She winked at me like you've got company, and disappeared into the house.

Bolt stood up with his usual practiced grace and reached into the pocket of his coat. What he pulled out caught me off guard—a folded piece of paper, yellowed at the corners, with a wax-sealed crease.

"Your father wanted you to have this," he said. "I said you'd been asking questions. He said it was time."

I took the letter from his hand like it was fragile, radioactive.

"I don't know what it says," Bolt added. "But I'd be willing to bet you'll find some of the answers you're looking for. Just remember... these are Maze's truths. Not yours."

Then, without fanfare, he stepped off the deck, got into his battle-scarred hover, and drove off like he was late for a revolution.

I stood there for a long moment, clutching the letter like it might vanish if I let it go. The paper was warm from Bolt's jacket, but there was something burning in my hands now. Something electric.

When I went inside, Mom was putting away dishes.

"Do you want to read this with me?" I asked. A part of me was afraid to open it alone.

She didn't even turn around. "The bond between a father and son is special," she said gently. "I love you both enough to respect the privacy of that. I hope you gain some clarity from it."

I went upstairs, closed the door behind me, and sat on my bed with the letter resting in my lap. I stared at it until the seal started to peel just from the heat of my fingers. Then, slowly, I opened it.

MAZE'S LETTER:

Dear Maigo,

By the time you read this, I'll probably be halfway across the Atlantic again—heading to some forgotten corner of the world, chasing ghosts and old dreams. But your face… your face stays with me wherever I go.

I heard you've been growing up fast. They say you've got your mother's stubborn grace and my irritating charm. Leigh told me you and Terra had… a moment. Don't worry. I gave him hell for telling me. But between you and me—there are worse things than loving someone with your whole heart. Be careful, be kind. And for god's sake, don't be stupid about it.

I've seen more of the world than most ever get the chance to. And let me tell you—it's a mess. But it's beautiful, too. I've eaten goat curry on a rooftop in Nairobi. Meditated in a red temple in Bhutan. Watched the sun bleed into the sea off a dock in Havana. But nothing—and I mean nothing —beats Jamaican oxtail with rice and peas. That dish alone might've been proof of God.

Now, I know you're tangled up in the V9 program. I've heard rumors. I've seen what it becomes. I won't lie to you, son—it scares the hell out of me.

But I also know that change doesn't only come from the outside.

Sometimes the only way to shift the gears of a machine is to climb inside it. You have a rare mind, Maigo. Sharp. Reflective. Stubborn, too. If you choose to walk the military path, then don't walk it blindly. Use it. Learn. Grow. Become so undeniably yourself that they can't ignore your voice. Earn their rank—and then use it to tear the walls down from the inside.

You don't owe me a promise. I'm not here to pull strings or shape your future like clay. I just want you to live fully. Live honestly. And wherever you end up, just make sure your soul belongs to you.

I love you.

—Dad

"Some believe that without divine presence things would not be this perfect.

Others believe that if things were not this perfect, they would not be."

(written in a hand that wasn't his)

I sat still for a long time. Omi's silence reminded me that I had to process this alone.

Reading it once wasn't enough. I read it three times, four. The words felt warm, then strange, then… distant.

I wanted it to be a map.

Instead, it was a compass—one that spun no matter which direction I faced.

I didn't know if I should take his advice. I didn't even know if he still knew me. Maybe the idea of me was easier to love than the truth of who I was becoming. I pressed the letter to my chest and laid back on the bed.

The silence wasn't so heavy now. Just waiting.

The next two weeks passed in a blur. Not fast—just... same.

The kind of stretch where you feel like you've been holding your breath the entire time. I kept waiting for something big to happen, like my world would suddenly spin again. But it didn't. It just ticked forward.

Every day looked like the one before it. I'd wake up late. My mom would already be up, making something in the kitchen and humming the tune of a song I hadn't heard since I was a kid. Sometimes we'd cook together. Sometimes we'd go out to a night market or one of the underground music halls where young artists played old instruments. Sometimes we'd just watch holo-flicks and pretend the rest of the world didn't exist.

I loved every moment of it.

Terra was okay. Jade kept me updated through brief messages. She said Leigh was keeping her under strict watch, still blaming me more than he probably should. I didn't try to force anything. Not yet. I just needed to know she was breathing. That she'd made it through.

Yoen called me every day. Sometimes just to tell me what he ate or complain about his dad's lectures on financial responsibility. Other times, we ended up on holo-chat watching terrible sci-fi movies from independent directors. He had a way of making things feel lighter without pretending they weren't heavy.

And then there was Omi.

Ever since I broke down beside my mother's hospital bed, he changed. Softer in tone. More character, more care. Like he'd finally recognized the weight I was carrying. Every night, he asked me questions—sometimes psychological, sometimes philosophical. Sometimes just *"what hurt the most today?"* He helped me patch up pieces of myself I hadn't even realized were cracked.

We rebuilt me. Slowly. Quietly.

The orientation syllabus for the summer program came in through my SatPad, and I read it more times than I care to admit. Each leg of the program was laid out with disturbingly cheerful language:

- **Combat Training** – "Real-world readiness for unexpected engagements."

- **Psychological Evaluation** – "Developing cognitive resiliency through exposure."

- **Tolerance and Resistance Conditioning** – No explanation, just a warning: "Clear your schedule. Prepare your mind."

- **Philosophy** – "Exploring the Doctrine of Order," which really meant Sylvain's worldview spoon-fed as gospel.

I wasn't naive enough to think any of this would be easy. Or clean. Or sane.

But I'd made peace with it. I'd decided that if I was going to do this, I'd catalog what mattered before I stepped inside.

Terra. My mother. My truth.

The letter. The twins. The train boy.

My questions. My pain.

My name.

Maigo.

I wasn't going to let them take that away from me.

The night before it all began, I sat in my room, staring at the empty walls and trying to imagine who I might become. A high-ranking military officer. One with enough power to debate Sylvain's decisions. An infamous beggar outlaw. One with enough influence to spark a real revolution. I was about to power down when a faint chime echoed through my telecoms link.

Incoming voice message. No ID. Encryption: Fail-safe protocol engaged.

I pressed play.

Her voice spilled out like wind through a crack in a window.

"Hey. It's me. Don't worry—I'm not gonna say anything I shouldn't. I know we're not supposed to talk." She paused, and I could hear the way her breath shook. "I just wanted to say good luck tomorrow. I know you'll do amazing things, even if I don't get to see them right now. I miss you, Maigo." Another pause. Longer. "I hope this isn't the end of our story. I hope… I hope there's still more to write."

The message ended. No return line.

I sat there, staring into the blue-black glow of my ceiling light, wondering if ghosts ever send you goodnight messages.

Chapter 8

SYLVAIN'S CHAMPION

I woke up with the weight of Terra's voice still ringing in my ears.

Good luck. I miss you. It was like a soft scar across my chest—sweet, but it stung every time I breathed.

I didn't respond. I couldn't. Not because I didn't want to, but because there was nothing I could say to her that wouldn't feel like a lie.

I dressed slow. My mother had left out one of my nicer uniforms, steamed and straightened, with a small note attached: **Be**

careful, but be great. She was gone when I came downstairs—already out for work—but her mug of cold tea still sat on the table, lipstick-stained and half full. The room's energy felt like a half-spoken wish.

They sent a shuttle to pick us up.

The drive to campus was quiet. Every hover passed like a shadow, and I watched them float by like they were all going somewhere I couldn't reach. The academy grounds were different from my high school. Tighter. Harsher. The guards were hardened—augmented, faceless, silent. The students were fewer, but they stood straighter, and paid closer attention. We weren't recruits anymore. We were assets in training.

I walked to the staging yard where the opening ceremony was held. The grass had been burned away and replaced with a titanium stage, wide enough to land a gunship. Above it, a holoscreen buzzed to life, and the Peacekeeper insignia shone bright enough to fry retinas. Rows of us lined up like chess pieces—juniors, seniors, and college-bound graduates. I could feel a tension beneath the surface of our skin, like someone had filled all of us with kerosene and was waiting to strike the match.

I didn't have to look to know Luna was nearby. I could feel her eyes on me like hot breath on the back of my neck. But I didn't turn. I didn't know what I'd say if I did. Every time I thought about Terra, I heard Luna's laugh echoing through the forest in the Russian simulation—and I just wasn't ready to face her.

Just before the official welcome began, Doctor Light and Doctor Cobb approached the stage. Cobb wore his usual polite smirk, but Light's face was stone. He looked like someone who had seen tomorrow and wasn't impressed.

Cobb addressed us, his voice amplified by a small impermanent augment on his throat. "Welcome to the V9 Summer Advancement Program," he said. "You've been selected not for who you are, but who you could become. You are the draft sketches of something greater—soldiers of peace, tools of progress, and, if you are worthy, architects of civilization itself." He paced, clasping his hands as usual. "Over the next three weeks, you'll be tested. Physically, mentally, morally. We will evaluate your tolerance to pain, your resistance to temptation, your psychological elasticity, and your ability to absorb and apply the principles of doctrine."

Sylvain's name wasn't said—but he was there in every word.

He continued. "You'll learn to quiet the part of your mind that flinches. You'll learn to walk through fire with your heart intact. And for those of you who succeed, the next step awaits." Cobb stopped, smiled. "Society thrives because we nurture the deserving. Earn your right."

The crowd was still.

"I wonder what the boy from the train would think of all this," I thought. *"All this ceremony for control. All this promise, built on who we can be, instead of who we already are. Where is the nurturing for the ones brave enough to be themselves?"*

No one clapped. There was no applause. We were dismissed in silence, ushered to our housing units, then to our training orientation. The program had begun.

The summer program wasn't about learning. It was about breaking you down fast enough that you wouldn't realize it was happening.

Day one started with a wake-up siren so loud I nearly hit my head on the ceiling of the bunk. By day three, I was already trained to jump out of bed with shoes laced and spine straight before Omi could even open his mouth.

"You know, Master Maigo, some of the other AIs in these quarters are having a very difficult time keeping their hosts in tact. I just wanted to say… I'm proud of you."

"Thanks," I muttered, brushing my teeth with a stick of paste that tasted like boiled plastic.

The routine was surgical. Formation. Drills. Strength training in hard-light arenas with low-gravity fields. Endless repetition, endless sweat. We weren't students anymore—we were machines in the making. There was no talking unless a drill instructor asked you something. No "how's your day," no "did you see that game last night," just eyes forward and a gut full of dirt.

Despite that, Luna kept finding ways to orbit me.

Sometimes it was subtle—a light elbow bump during weight training, a glance when they called us into the hall for orientation check-ins. Other times, it was direct.

We were jogging laps around the outer perimeter of the campus dome. My calves were on fire and the cold wind made my sweat feel like acid, but Luna caught up beside me anyway.

She paced quietly for a few steps, then said, breathlessly, "You still mad at me?"

I didn't look at her. "I'm not anything at you."

She laughed. "That's so muchworse."

We ran in silence for a bit longer, the sound of our boots muffled by the padded training track. When we rounded the next bend, the dome lights cast a long, slow shadow between us.

"You were right," she said.

I glanced at her. "About what?"

"I do try to manipulate people." Her voice wasn't sarcastic or mocking. Just… hollow. "But not because I'm evil or whatever. It's… something else."

I slowed my pace slightly. She did too.

"My dad used to hit me when I got things wrong," she said suddenly. "Not all the time, but enough. If I spilled a drink, took too long in the bathroom, or even had an opinion that didn't come from him—boom, backhand. Every time I failed, I became unlovable. Unsafe."

I didn't speak. I didn't know what to say.

"So I stopped failing," she said. "Started being… whoever people wanted me to be. I learned how to get people to like me. Because being liked meant being safe."

I stopped running completely. She did too. We stood in the red-tinted light, sweat steaming off our skin like fog.

"Why are you telling me this?" I asked.

"Because I think it's time I stop lying. At least to you."

I looked at her—really looked at her. She wasn't performing anymore. No fake smile, no flirtatious tilt to her hips. Just a scared girl, stripped bare in a place that punished vulnerability.

"I'm not gonna judge you," I said. "But I also don't think I can be what you want me to be. I just have a lot going on right now."

She nodded. "I figured."

"But I can be your friend," I added.

That caught her off guard. Her eyes glassed over, then she blinked them dry. "Okay."

We started walking again, slower this time, the other cadets vanishing ahead of us on the track. I didn't know what came next. But in that moment, I think we both felt something lift.

Not a romance. Not a betrayal. Just a fragile truth between two broken kids trying to survive.

After basic physical training, the real program began.

I lost track of the days almost immediately.

No clocks, no windows. Just the sterile hum of artificial morning, over and over again. Fresh air leaking through cracked doors was like a drug.

Combat Training.

Day one, I fought a boy named Silas—taller, older, with wrists like broken tree trunks. He disarmed me in seconds and slammed me to the mat hard enough to rattle the bones in my spine.

"Again," the instructor barked.

Silas grinned.

Day two, I was faster. Not better. Just faster. I landed a shot to his ribs. Got a nod from the watching AI. Got my lip split open in return. I remember the taste.

Blood feels more real in simulation than in life.

Day three, I pinned him. A full six seconds. My ribs hurt when I laughed that night.

Psych Eval.

We weren't in a room. We were in the depths of my subconscious mind.

Everything was black, except for a red chair and a screen that looked like a mirror but wasn't. A solid concrete room with invasive acoustics. The voice came from nowhere and everywhere. It felt longer than it was.

"Let's talk about your mother's overdose.."

I didn't move.

"Let's talk about your father's absence.."

Silence.

"Let's talk about Luna. About Terra. About the little girl in the river.."

I clenched my fists.

"Emotions are transient," the voice said. "You are not your pain."

The screen flickered. I saw myself crying. Then I saw nothing.

Tolerance/Resistance.

This was the worst.

Sensory deprivation chamber. Water tank. Naked mind.

Once, I think they played the sound of my mother screaming my name—just once—followed by five straight hours of silence.

A needle floated up to me from the endless abyssal water surrounding me. Same model I found on our kitchen floor.

A message blinked across the wall:
"Make it stop."

My screams were muffled by the sheer size of the chamber.

It echoed forever.

Philosophy.

We sat in a dome. Curved black walls, no edges. One by one, we filed in and sat cross-legged on warm, carbon-tiled ground. In walked a master of oration.

Veritas was beautiful. Perfect skin. Silver eyes. Spoke like poetry. "There is no meaning in suffering unless you assign it one," it said. "Your pain is not special. You are not special. You are replaceable. That is your strength."

Everyone nodded.

The boy next to me cried, silently.

I looked around. Every face was still. No blinking. No questions.

Veritas' eloquence far outweighed the propaganda he spoke. He masterfully weaved infallible truths with Sylvain's teachings. Opaque intentions. Entrancing diction. He could've told me I was a baby owl and I probably would've hooted a few times before I asked any questions.

By the end of the fourth day, I couldn't remember what Terra's voice sounded like when she was happy. Just the post-suicidal rasp.

I started repeating things to myself just to keep some version of me alive.

The words of the boy on the subway: *"The only sin is inauthenticity."*

The first time Luna kissed me. Her expertise in intimacy birthed maturity in me.

The night Terra threw that girl in the water.

The morning after.

Each lesson felt like someone was carving pieces out of me.

Putting something artificial in their place.

And I just kept going back.

Later that night, I sat alone in my dorm cube, the lights off, Omi mercifully silent. I opened my recording software and stared at the blinking cursor for ten minutes before finally hitting "Record."

"Hey, Terra." My voice cracked on the first word. I cleared my throat and tried again. "I don't know if I'll ever send this. But there are some things I need to say. The summer program is… hell. Every day feels like I'm being torn apart and reassembled in someone else's image. They're trying to make us unbreakable, and I think that's the same thing as making us forget how to feel."

I paused, rewound the message, deleted it, started over.

The next time I kept going. "I wanted to tell you I still think about the forest. The dog. Your voice when you said 'I love you.' I should've said it back. I should've done a lot of things differently. But I didn't. And I can't change that now." I took a breath. "I don't know who I'm becoming. But I remember who I was when I was with you. And that version of me… he felt worth something."

I stopped the recording. Sat in the dark for a long time, listening to myself sigh.

"Omi, search the V9 archives. Pull up the internment camp."

A grainy freeze-frame of Terra's body in the snow. Her limbs twisted. Blood painting the white ground like calligraphy.

I hit play.

The dog. Her scream. My hesitation. Her words. The bite.

I watched it all.

And then I watched it again.

And again.

Our big test was the next day, but I watched it deep into the night. I didn't stop until my eyes got heavy. Some twilight-zone version of it played in my nightmares.

I could still feel the adrenaline the next morning.

Dr. Cobb's voice was colder than usual when he summoned us. "This will be your final test," he announced, his face carved from stone. "Do not look for meaning. There is none beyond performance."

The chamber was huge—far bigger than I expected. Lined with tall white tanks, each filled with an eerie blue fluid. Floating inside them were faceless synthetic bodies—some male, some female, some barely human. It looked like a graveyard for forgotten mannequins.

"These are bio-synthetic shells," Cobb said. "You will control them from your V9 chambers for the next series of tasks. Your real bodies will remain safely under anesthesia. You should view and treat the shells like your own. Survival fuels ambition." Even he knew to let us digest that for a moment. "Let's begin."

TASK ONE: The Vase

The synthetic body booted up instantly. I was sitting in a minimalist living room—three chairs arranged in a triangle. Across from me sat three strangers. Holograms, I realized quickly. Each one hyper-realistic.

Behind them was a shattered vase.

The first one, a young man with a twitch in his left eye, pointed to the woman on his right. "She did it. I saw her knock it over."

The woman gasped. "Liar! He did it. He was throwing a ball inside and it slipped."

The third one, an older man, held his palms up. "You're both wrong. I did it. I dropped it when I was cleaning."

All three provided different evidence. A ball on the floor. A broom leaning on the wall. A smear of fingerprints on a nearby counter.

They watched me, waiting for a verdict.

"There's no obvious answer," I thought. *"But someone's lying. There's something I'm missing."*

I replayed each statement in my head, catching small details. The woman said the boy was throwing a ball, but he said he saw her knock it over. If he saw her, how was he throwing the ball?

I spoke carefully. "You. The one with the twitch. You're lying."

The holograms froze. Then disappeared.

A tone rang out. **"Correct."**

Later, I overheard Max arguing with another recruit.

"It wasn't the woman?" Max said, confused. "She was the only one who mentioned the ball."

"She was being framed," I interjected.

Max shook his head. "No way you figured it out. Lucky guess."

I didn't answer him.

I wasn't guessing.

TASK TWO: The Burning House

They placed a virtual child in my care.

A girl. Five or six. Braided hair and scared eyes. She reached for my hand immediately. "Can we go now? I don't want to be late for school.." she asked.

We walked through a small suburban sim —silent but for the sounds of birds and distant sirens.

Halfway to the school building, we passed a burning house. Flames licking the windows. An old woman screamed from inside, coughing violently.

Jade, a few streets over with her own synthetic child, didn't hesitate. She bolted toward the house.

"No!" someone shouted.

The house exploded inward as she stepped inside. A wave of flame engulfed her shell. Her child was left standing alone in the street.

I froze.

The girl tugged on my hand. "What's that noise?" she asked.

I looked down at her. "Nothing we need to worry about," I lied.

I kept walking.

Later, they showed us replays.

Jade sat in silence as Cobb lectured.

"You sacrificed your mission to indulge in fantasy," he told her.

She didn't argue.

TASK THREE: The Dive Bar

It looked like a twentieth century dump on the edge of nowhere. Flickering neon signs, barstools older than time, fake wood paneling stained with sweat and beer.

Yoen was waiting inside. So was the objective.

"Last one standing," said a gruff synthetic voice over the intercom. "No rules."

Yoen cracked his neck. "Been waiting for this."

He moved fast. Always did. Threw a stool at me. I ducked, rolled behind the bar. Grabbed a broken bottle. He came over the top, swinging a cue stick.

I slashed. He cursed. Dropped the stick and grabbed a frying pan from the bar's kitchen window. Swung it like a sword.

I blocked it with a chair leg, barely holding my ground. He drove his weight into me, and we crashed into the wall, glass raining down on our heads.

It went like that for almost ten minutes. Raw. Desperate. Like we both needed to bleed just to feel something again.

In the end, I disarmed him by shoving his hand into a boiling deep fryer. He screamed, and I punched him into unconsciousness.

The system buzzed. **"Victory: Maigo."**

Back in my real body, I woke up nauseous. It wasn't like the simulations in the classroom. My hands trembled like they remembered everything the synthetic ones had done.

I looked across the chamber at the others waking up. Some were crying. Jade was stone-faced. Yoen refused to look at me.

Cobb clapped once, slow and theatrical. "Well done, everyone. We've got everything we need."

I didn't feel victorious. I felt like someone had handed me a mask and told me to forget I ever had a face.

The training facility was unusually quiet.

No cheering. No congratulations. Just the soft hum of cleaning drones gliding across the black marble floor, erasing any trace of the shell trials. I walked past a line of recruits still nursing the psychological bruises left behind in their wake. Jade sat with her arms wrapped around her knees. Yoen still wouldn't meet my eyes.

As I passed through the final scanner gate, Dr. Cobb appeared beside me like a glitch in

the system.

"Mr. Rizen," he said, his voice clipped. "You've been given special commendation for your performance. You're to report immediately to chamber 9-Sigma."

Odd.

"Isn't 9-Sigma in the restricted wing?" I asked.

Cobb didn't answer. He was already turning away.

Omi's voice rang in my ear, low and alert. *"Something's wrong, Master Maigo. This isn't written anywhere in the program syllabus."*

"I know," I thought. But I kept walking.

The hallway narrowed as I neared the restricted wing. Everything here was sleek, soundless. Even the lights felt like they were watching me—more surveillance than illumination.

Omi crackled in again. *"You do not have to do this. You can leave. You have earned enough favor to walk away."*

I stood in the doorway, the silence swelling around me like a vacuum.

"I have to know," I whispered.

Chapter 9

A MOMENT WITH MASTER

T he room was colder than I expected. One V9 chest. No lights. No Cobb or Light to greet me. Just a matte-black chamber sitting in the center. My reflection stared back at me in its obsidian shell, wide-eyed and unsure.

They said Sylvain wanted to meet with me.

Of course, it had to be a simulation—there's no way the Atlas General would risk setting foot near a recruit, not even one with special marks. I hovered my hand over the latch, hesitating just long enough to wonder if I was walking into a trap.

I settled into the chamber. The door slid shut on its own. I could hear a locking mechanism engage.

The moment I closed my eyes, my breath scratched the dryness in my throat.

My hands trembled as I placed them on the control rests. The inside was too quiet. Too sterile.

Even the boot sequence sounded different—deeper tones, no interface display. A black screen.

I closed my eyes.

"Initializing private channel…"

Blackout.

I opened my eyes to sunlight. Warm, gold, unapologetic sunlight spilling across a pristine lake and bouncing off the mirrored surface of the water. Birds chirped, unbothered. Pines stood tall in the distance, hugging the edge of the tree-line like protectors of some sacred truth. The house behind me was nothing special. A timber cabin, roof angled to catch the sun. Earthy. Quiet. Unsettlingly peaceful.

Then I saw him.

Sylvain was dragging a carcass up the gravel driveway—a deer. Blood trailed behind it, painting streaks of red onto the rocks. His shirt was half-unbuttoned and flecked with crimson. He didn't look presidential. Not like the man I'd seen on massive screens in Los Mitos or the polished visage broadcast during global addresses. Here, he looked… normal.

"Welcome to my sanctuary, Maigo!" he called, hoisting the animal by its hind legs.

His voice had a strange warmth to it. Not theatrical. Not demanding. More like an uncle you'd never met before, but who acted like he'd known you your whole life.

"Could you give me a hand?" he asked, as if I hadn't been standing there in shock.

I stepped forward slowly. The gravel crunched beneath my feet like tiny bones. When I reached him, he handed me one of the legs, and together we lifted the deer onto a wooden bleeding rack.

He pulled a knife from his belt and without hesitation, slit the jugular. Blood gushed down into a silver bucket below with an audible slosh. The scent hit me a second later—metallic and wet.

"The Jews really had some good points, you know," he said casually, wiping his blade on a cloth. "Kosher really is better. Clean bloodletting. No adrenaline in the meat."

I blinked. I had no idea how to respond to that.

"My father was Christian," he continued, peeling back the skin with practiced ease. "That's where I got my work ethic."

I wanted to ask why he was telling me this. Why he was acting like this wasn't the most powerful man in the world meeting a 16-year-old kid. But I didn't say anything. I just watched him work—watched the steam rise from the deer's warm flesh as he pulled the hide off.

"I grew up with this," he went on. "Chores, sermons, pain. A man worth anything should be able to feed himself. That's how you build character. That's how you build resolve." The knife slid down the muscle like he was painting with it. "That's the problem with you kids. You're being taught to feel before you're taught to suffer. It makes you weak. You ever shot anything? Never mind." He held up two steaks, perfectly cut from the haunch. "Would you like to come inside?"

The cabin smelled like cedar and smoke. Cast iron pans hung above the stove, and sunlight streamed in through windows lined with hand-blown glass. It wasn't techy. No screens. No automation. Just wood, stone, and steel.

He laid the steaks on a cutting board and reached for oil and salt. "I know quite a bit about you, Maigo. We've kept an eye out for a long time." He glanced at me from the corner of his eye. "You're the rebellious type. Can't take no for an answer. Bleed for what you believe in, right?" He clicked the burner on. A halo of blue flame flared beneath the skillet. "I know you're also not sure what you believe. It's hard to pair that victim stance with determinism." He sneered. "Sorry. Let's start over. This is your time. Most people never get this opportunity. Is there anything you'd like to ask me?"

My thoughts split in two. One half screamed "*ask if he knows about dad!*" The other clawed at the bigger question. I knew what he wanted. He was picking a fight. Putting me in my place. I could feel it behind the way he handled that knife—measured, assured, almost like he was carving my skin.

Finally, I said, "What made you stop believing?"

Sylvain actually paused. The oil crackled. He looked impressed. "Experimentation," he said. He walked over to the dining room and gestured to an open Bible on the table, already turned to a chapter labeled 'Genesis.' "I read that. Front to back. Memorized it, even. As a child, I believed. Wholeheartedly. But then I started to test it." He ran a fingertip down the open page. "'In the beginning, God created the heavens and the earth...'" He glanced at me. "But what if you're the one doing the creating?" He sat down. "I discovered something, Maigo. The one-to-one ratio of my choices to my outcomes. When I acted, things changed. When I didn't, they didn't. Cause. Effect. The pattern was too perfect. No mystery. No divine interference. Just me. I became the creator in my story." He smiled. "A god, if you will."

I swallowed the bittersweet taste of confirmation.

He stood again and flipped the steaks. "It's like riding a dragon through a sea of possibility," he said. "Some people hold the reins. Some people let go. Want to know who let go?" He didn't wait for an answer. "Junkies. So afraid to confront their plight that they'd rather melt their consciousness away. Hopeless dreamers. Too lazy to take action. Genuinely believing their desires might fall from the sky. My father." He stopped moving. "Heart disease. The doctors said they could save him. He said God would save him. So he died. And left my mother to drown in grief while he floated away in delusion." The tear that rolled down his cheek sizzled when it hit the hot skillet. "But that wasn't why I did what I did," he said. "That was just the moment I knew."

I leaned forward. "Then... why take away our choice? Why outlaw religion?"

Sylvain took the steaks off the pan and placed one on my plate. He sat across from me and folded his hands just like Dr. Cobb.

"Because religion hurt too many people."

And he began to list them:

- Anti-vaxx parents whose children died.

- Rape victims forced to carry trauma in their wombs.

- Tithes stolen to fuel a pastor's affair with greed.

- Children sexually abused in silence behind rosaries.

- Suicide bombers killing in the name of piety.

"I believed in freedom of choice," he said, voice low. "But what kind of leader allows people to make the objectively wrong choice?"

He explained how he climbed through government ranks by writing policies to help the underserved—reducing poverty, increasing access to care, ending religious monopolies on public policy. He described how the Vatican and its allied resistance declared war.

"How could they resist the good I was doing?" His face hardened. "So I ended it. I won. And I made sure it would never happen again."

For the first time, I saw something fragile behind the tyrant. Something wounded. And maybe… something just.

Then he said, "Join me."

I looked up, in awe.

"Work for me. You're smart. Gifted. You've seen both sides. I have an elite unit of intelligence operatives—undercover, independent, powerful. You'd be perfect." He leaned forward. "I'll give you everything you need to shape this world. All I ask is that you help me save it."

The steak on my plate had gone cold. I stared at the perfect sear lines and the soft pink center like I was trying to find an answer in the fibers of meat. Sylvain, for all his precision, was dead silent—waiting. I could feel it in the weight of his gaze, even though he hadn't looked at me since his offer.

I set down my fork. "Sir…"

Sylvain's fingers twitched.

I bowed. "I want to thank you for the opportunity," I said, choosing each word like it was a mine I might step on. "But I can't accept."

The air seemed to crystallize around us.

I continued, assuring humility in my tone.

"I'm sixteen. I'm still figuring out who I am, what I believe—hell, I'm just trying to survive school, spend time with my mom, chase a girl, maybe even fall in love."

Sylvain looked up slowly.

"I'm flattered," I added. "Really. But I can't fight or kill for something I don't fully understand. I'd rather spend my time becoming someone worth trusting, than faking it to meet expectations I didn't set."

There it was. My truth, naked on the table.

Sylvain blinked. Once. With a long pause in the eyelid-down position. "Unacceptable," he said flatly.

He stood from the table with a grace so slow it felt rehearsed. Then he picked up a mirror from the sideboard—polished, oval, no frame. He held it like a priest holds communion.

"You," he began, voice coiling like smoke. "A teenage boy looked in the face of your world's ultimate power and had the arrogance to believe I'd let you say no."

I felt my body stiffen.

He walked toward me, each step heavy, purposeful. "My favorite thing about free will," he said, "is that I can impose mine over yours." He set the mirror on the table in front of me.

"Look."

I did.

It wasn't me. The face of my shell stared back at me with pity. Scared for the both of us. Trying not to shake. Trying to remember how to breathe.

Sylvain's tone softened—but somehow that made it worse. "Listen, child. You are not free. You will never be free. You are bound by the chains of attachment. And you are too cowardly to break them." He circled behind me. "Did you ever consider what might happen to your mother if I placed her in a cold, dark cell where no one could hear her scream? Or if Terra's young, delicate life was cut short because of your decision? Her blood would be on your hands—do you think you'd survive that?"

I stood up, fists clenched, heart pounding.

He laughed. Softly. "Are you so important in your own mind, that you never once wondered if I've been inching you toward this table from the very beginning?"

He walked to the window. The lake outside was still glistening, but it looked different now—foreign. Unsafe.

"You weren't chosen, Maigo. You were sculpted. I am the puppet master you seek." He turned to me slowly. "Maigo Rizen," he said, pronouncing my last name like a sentence. "Son of Maze, the traveling prophet. The antithesis to my will."

That was when everything clicked.

The suspicious recruitment.

Colonel Haines' manipulation.

The summer program.

Everything.

"You're all I need," Sylvain said, "to destroy him."

My chest collapsed inward. I glanced at the sky, the trees, the table—looking for an exit.

Sylvain saw it. "Ah, yes. It has finally become clear for you," he grinned. "You are still in the V9 system. And I am the one holding the key. You cannot leave without my permission."

I swallowed the bile in my throat.

He stepped toward me and placed a hand on my shoulder. "You've lost. Accept your fate, young beggar."

My voice came out raw. "What do you want from me?"

He leaned in, and for the first time, I saw what lay behind his eyes—absolute conviction, cold and immovable. "You will remain in this pod," he whispered. "Your body will be preserved. But out there in the world, this bio-synthetic shell will carry your consciousness."

My eyes dampened at the realization of my fate.

"You will infiltrate the FPM," he continued, "and you will track down your father."

Tears came next. A flood.

"You will gain his trust," Sylvain said. "You will walk among his people and bring me everything I need to end their twisted legacy once and for all."

I'd never felt so much hatred for someone.

His smile returned, razor-sharp.

"Welcome to your prison, Maigo."

AUTHOR

J. B. Jefferson is an African American, self-taught, writer. He grew up in Saint Louis, MO with his mother and older brother. Despite the obstacles of poverty, he was able to graduate college and earn a degree in sociology. He currently works for the Missouri Department of Social Services, rehabilitating criminal adolescents. His work and upbringing are the primary sources of his writing inspiration. He believes that creative outlets are essential to a healthy mind.

"If you can imagine a better world, you should write about it." – J. B. Jefferson

www.ingramcontent.com/pod-product-compliance
Lightning Source LLC
Chambersburg PA
CBHW070555260626
47161CB00002B/612